1 MADE OF NO

Sadie

"NO," Kate says when I hold up the tiny jeans. "No pants. No."

Of course she refuses them. She's two. Two-year-olds are made of No. But I have to be at work in forty minutes, it's a fifteen-minute drive, and I need some time built into the schedule for me to have a complete and total breakdown.

Today will be the girls' first time at daycare, even though I swore this day would never come. I didn't want my girls to be marched out of their own home every morning like tiny nine-to-fivers. I wanted them to enjoy the comforts of home through those formative early years, so I could control their environment. You know, for optimal brain development and health.

Yet here we are. Daycare. If motherhood has taught me anything, it's that nothing is truly in my control.

And it's all because this family has had a spot of trouble with nannies. When I say a "spot of trouble" I'm underplaying things just a little bit. The first nanny decided that boinking my ex-husband was a good idea. And yes, I know the nanny and Decker were equally culpable.

But that was only the beginning of the Great Nanny Hell Spiral. Nannies number two, three, and four quit within weeks. They were poached by other playgroup mothers who didn't have twins. And nanny number five lasted four months, until I realized she'd been stealing from me the entire time.

The fates have decided that employing nannies was not for me. After I discovered three grand in unauthorized credit card charges, daycare suddenly sounded like a reasonable option, and my kiddos' developing personalities might even benefit from more social interaction.

Kate's pants are now the only obstacle to this new plan.

I take a deep breath and pray for patience. Then I let it out again. I am a trained therapist. An expert in psychology. Insight into the human mind is my specialty. Yet my years of education are no match for negotiating with my toddlers. "You can't go to school without pants on," I point out. "It's a rule."

"No pants," she repeats, just in case I didn't get it the first time. "No no no."

"Fine," I lie. "Leggings instead. Gotcha." I open up her dresser drawer and grab a pair of purple leggings. They'll look ridiculous with her green T-shirt, but it's better than a meltdown.

Anything is better than a meltdown. My meltdown this time, not hers.

She regards the leggings with round-cheeked suspicion.

"Please put these on," I whisper. "We can't have waffles until they're on." I hate bribing my child with food, but there's no denying its effectiveness. Faster than you can say *organic maple syrup* she toddles over and offers a chubby little leg for the cladding.

"Well done!" I say with false cheer. Scooping her into the leggings and then onto my hip, I lift both of us off the floor and look around for her sister. Amy is sitting beside the baby gate, waiting for us, ever-present pacifier in her mouth and Piggypoo clutched in her chubby hand.

She's my cooperative child. And I tremble at the thought of trying to leave her to the chaos of daycare.

———

Twenty minutes later I walk them both through the door at Small Packages daycare. I'm carrying a duffel bag full of extra clothes, nut-free food, and comforting items from home. The most comforting item, in my opinion, is the lengthy instructional letter I've included. I've written a long list of descriptions of the twins' varying emotional reactions, complete with solutions. They'll need the pacifier and Piggypoo to soothe Amy. And there's a football helmet to ensure Kate doesn't hurt herself too badly when tackling things. I've jotted down the songs they like and a list of foods that will send them into a tailspin.

Next week I'll drop off some suggested reading on childcare development. I don't want to come off too strong on day one.

Even though I've been preparing for this moment, my heart rate is still about twice the healthy limit. Because I know when I walk out of here Amy will lose her mind. And even Kate will take a break from trying to run the world and hate me for leaving her.

I turn my critical eye onto the ponytailed girl behind the reception desk. She looks about sixteen years old. And she's in charge of checking kids in and out? Seriously? What do these people know about security?

My stomach dives for the tenth time today. No moment in parenting has ever made me feel guiltier. Not even when I fell down the stairs carrying Kate. (She was fine, but it was close!) And not even when my girls ask, "Where Daddy go?" and I have no answer to give them.

At least that's his fault, not mine.

But today is all on me. This feels like dropping the girls off at the county jail. What if Amy misplaces Piggypoo or needs a drink of water? Will someone bring her one? I won't see them for nine hours. *Nine*. Entire civilizations have fallen in less time than that.

"Good morning! Welcome to Small Packages! You must be Sadie! And Kate and Amy!"

I blink at Miss Ponytail, surprised that she got that right. "We are. Yes. First day. Here we go!" My words are the equivalent of machine gun speech—nervous and rapid-fire.

"Here is your welcome packet, complete with webcam access." She pushes a shiny folder across the desk at me. "Step right over to the ladybug room! He's waiting for you."

Kate takes off running toward the door with the ladybugs crawling all over it. But Amy wraps her arms around my knee. "No school," she says softly. "Home now."

Oh boy. I feel my throat beginning to double in size. Here comes the tearful departure. I know a woman whose daughter cried at the daycare door every day for three years. This could be bad. My daughter is going to end up in therapy because I leave her every day to give therapy to others.

Where is the logic in that?

I scoop Amy off the floor and nuzzle her silky cheek. "They have toys in there," I whisper. "If you don't try out school, you won't get to see the toys. Hey, I see a really great rocking horse in the corner." It's the plush kind with a silky mane.

Even so, pointing it out makes me the worst kind of traitor. Amy is my sensitive one. My parents call her an Indigo Child, but I don't like to influence her with their new-agey wisdom. It is true that Amy only wants her mother, which I'm both proud and guilty about. I mean, here I'm trying to sell her down the river for a fake pony ride. When she gets off that horse five minutes from now, her mommy will be *gone*.

It's suddenly very hard to swallow.

I try to loosen Amy's death grip around my neck.

These miserable thoughts are interrupted by a very jolly, very male voice. "Sadie Mathews?"

I look up to see a startlingly gorgeous man seated just inside the ladybug doorway. He's young—in his twenties, probably—with tanned skin and wavy brown hair. He has smooth, very muscular arms. They *bulge*. His biceps are straining the sleeves of the polo shirt he's wearing. They're fascinating. I didn't know that muscles could ripple like that.

He clears his throat.

Giving myself a mental slap, I straighten my spine and get back to the program at hand. It's time to betray my children and make a quick exit.

But then I meet Mr. Biceps' gaze, and find something in it that's a bit familiar. I can't put my finger on why, though.

"Wow, Sadie!" His smile is so wide that the tickle of familiarity intensifies. "It's been too long! And are these your daughters?"

"Y-yes?" I stammer. Who *is* this guy? I've seen those warm, blue eyes before. I think. But the rest of him isn't familiar at all. There's no way I could know a man this attractive and not remember him.

I may be divorced, but I'm not dead.

"Hi," I try, giving him a big, familiar handshake and a smile. "How are you?"

His eyes narrow. Then he stands up, covering his heart with one broad palm. "I'm trying really hard here not to be crushed that you don't remember me. But it's more than a little heart-breaking. I'm Liam McAllister. I know it's been a while, but..."

"Oh my God, *Liam!*" My poor, stressed-out little brain tries to make sense of all the contrary information. "But... You're six feet tall!" The last time I saw Liam McAllister we were the same height. Also, he was a pimply fourteen-year-old.

"I'm actually 6-3!" He beams, and then I recognize those dimples. Liam was always such a sweet little boy. But, Lordy. I'm experiencing a moment of cognitive dissonance trying to reconcile the Liam I used to babysit with this hunk of man.

"Seriously, I need a ladder just to shake your hand. What are they feeding you?"

"Aw!" He leans forward and literally picks me—and therefore Amy, too—off the ground for a quick hug. As if we weigh nothing. "It's awfully good to see you. You look exactly the same."

"Nice try," I mutter under my breath, because I know that's a lie. Since my divorce, when I look in the mirror, I see a stressed-out, unattractive woman. And just so you don't think it's all in my head, my ex made sure to tell me that he wasn't attracted to me anymore. And that it was my fault he strayed.

"And, wow. Your daughters! Twins! I don't think the world can really handle two beautiful Sadie clones. I'm surprised there isn't, like, a disruption in the magnetic field at the poles." He sits down again. "What is your name, miss?" Liam addresses this question to Kate. He's taken her hand in his, and it's the only thing preventing her from tearing into the room to start rooting through the toys.

"Kate," she chirps.

"I'm Liam. You look like you want to hit that dress-up box, right?"

She nods like a thoroughbred in the starting gates at the Kentucky Derby.

"Have at it then." He releases her, and I grab ahold of her green shirt before she can pounce.

"Hat!" I say. Kate grabs the little football helmet from the duffel bag, shoves it on her head, and charges, where I know she's going to *literally* hit that dress-up box head-on.

"Sensory issues?" he asks, but it's soft and not judgey.

"We're navigating it," I respond, a little startled that he seems to get it.

"No worries. The dress-up box is cardboard. She'll be just fine. We also have a climbing wall outside on the play structure."

I try to nod, but it's hard to do with a two-year-old boa-constrictored around your neck.

Liam drops his voice to a softer timbre. "You must be Amy."

She stares at him. At the bulging muscles, maybe, or perhaps that's just me. Slowly I lower her to the floor, and she doesn't complain. She's sucking on that pacifier so vigorously that I'm relieved not to be breastfeeding anymore. She tips her head to the side, as if considering whether Liam-Who-Grew-Into-a-Hunk will be her new bestie.

Liam makes a beckoning motion to me, and for a split second I think he's asking me to sit in his lap. I'm giving the invitation some serious consideration when I realize that he means for me to pass the duffel bag to him.

I hand it over.

"Amy, listen," he says, never taking his kind eyes off hers. "There is a train set with enough track to go all the way around the snack table." He gives her a meaningful nod. "I was thinking of setting it up, but I'm gonna need some help. Are you in?"

My daughter pops her pacifier out, says "Piggypoo?" and then plunks the pacifier back in. I'm just about to explain when Liam sets the duffel bag down and rescues Piggypoo from its dark depths. He holds it out to her and she gives him a solemn nod. She takes it from him and nestles it securely under her armpit.

He holds out a hand slowly, palm up, the way you'd gain the trust of a dog.

She puts her little hand in the center of his.

"All right. We'd better get to work, then."

I'm mesmerized as Amy takes a few steps closer. She's standing right against his knee, looking up at him admiringly.

Liam glances at me. *Go*, he mouths.

I turn on my heel and beat it out of there.

2 MIMOSAS & HOT MEN

Sadie

"HERE'S to two full weeks of the kiddos in daycare!" Ash says.
The three of us raise our mimosas toward the clear June morning
sky and toast.

My girlfriends and I are sitting on my big front porch, possibly
for the first time since Decker left. Bit by bit I'm reclaiming my
single life, and putting a single woman's stamp on my home. I've
put pillows on every piece of lawn furniture just to spite my ex.

Decker hated pillows. That's a sign, right? I should have
known there was something off about him.

"Goddammit, I want some real alcohol," Brynn says and rubs
her gigantic eight-month pregnant belly. "A mimosa without
bubbly isn't a mimosa. It's a disappointment."

"When that...you know..." Ash motions to Brynn's belly, "*thing*
in you is born, I will bring you the biggest martini ever," Ash says.
"You've earned it."

"It's not a thing," I remind her. "It's a baby." Ash is not the
maternal sort.

"Whatever. It's a little person with gums. It's horrifying." She actually shivers.

"Which reminds me," Brynn says, "I have some questions about breastfeeding."

"Okay! One of my favorite topics. Hit me." I've done extensive research into the values of maternal bonding, and I also have real-world experience nursing twins.

Ash holds up her hands. "No. Nope. Uh-uh. We are not going down that road. You two can meet up and talk about all things maternal, but when it's the three of us, we are nipple-conversation free. I mean, I've already compromised by showing up here at 9:30 in the morning on a Saturday. This is as much adulting as I can take for at least a few hours."

"Nipple free, huh?" I ask. And Brynn's eyes sparkle, because she knows this trick, too. "*Braht*" I say slowly. "Braht..."

Ash scowls and then covers up her nipples, which go immediately erect every time she thinks of her boyfriend.

Brynn and I high-five each other. "It's the best party trick ever!" Brynn giggles.

"I hate you. Both of you," Ash says. But she doesn't mean it.

We sit in silence for a moment, listening to the birdsong. I close my eyes and let the sun warm my skin. It'll be hot today, but right now it's just perfect. My street is quiet, except for the sound of wind gently rustling the leaves.

I'm glad I stood my ground during the divorce, when Decker and his girlfriend made a play to keep this house. But my daughters need constancy and a steady routine. They only have one parent who provides it, and I can provide it best right here in this house.

Even if money is a little tight.

"I want to propose a toast," Ash says, lifting her glass. "Here's to Sadie finally jumping into the dating world again!"

I lift my glass as a reflex and then immediately wish I hadn't.

"Yeah, baby!" Brynn whoops, and I feel ambushed. This morning is supposed to be relaxing, and this isn't a relaxing topic. I take a really big gulp of my mimosa and try to forget that Ash brought it up.

"You gotta hit that," Ash adds, "and report back."

My mimosa goes down the wrong pipe, and I start coughing. "I'm not *hitting* anything," I wheeze. "It's just a coffee date."

"But you're meeting him at a restaurant, right? After work?" Brynn asks.

"Sure, but I'm just going to order coffee." The truth is that I'd rather stay home and sand the calluses off my feet. The idea of making small talk on a date makes me want to curl up in a ball and rock. But it's time, I think. I need to get back out there just to prove to myself I can.

Lately my life has been just work and parenting. Ash is busy with Braht, and Tom and Brynn are nesting like a couple of rabid beavers. I need to have a life beyond Netflix alone in my jammies. It's not like I'm trying to relive my youth. I don't expect to go clubbing, or take a flying trapeze class.

But I'm lonely. I need adult conversation.

I wish my sister Megan lived here instead of all the way in Atlanta.

"Sadie, honey," Ash says. "You can't go out with a guy to a restaurant and order coffee. You need to have a full meal. Have a drink. Have' fun. Maybe it'll be super hot and you'll end up all pinned against a wall and writhing in delight and..."

"His name is Earl."

That stops Ash cold. "What?"

"My date. His name is Earl. He's my receptionist's half-brother. He's from Marquette. Apparently he likes deer hunting and making homemade jerky."

"Homemade jerky?" Brynn perks up. "That's a thing? Can you get me the recipe?"

"Earl?" Ash repeats, ignoring Brynn. "This is who you're dating?" I can hear the pity in her voice.

"Well, I've got to start somewhere. Don't I? And it's not like I was meeting anyone on that singles app."

"That's because you never filled out your profile," Ash reminds me. "Asking men to pay you a $25 application fee before you'll give them your name and picture does not send a message of warmth and availability."

I think it sends the perfect message. I want my profile to weed out anyone who wasn't going to take me seriously. Basically, I want to just weed out *everyone*.

Suddenly I'm thirsty for more mimosas. "We need something else to toast to," I say.

This is honestly the first time I've felt relaxed in forever, and I don't want to ruin it with thoughts of Earl. The girls are with their dad and my BFFs are here. I have the whole morning and afternoon to relax. Brynn has fed us homemade cream puffs and bacon. The only time I eat gluten is when she cooks for us, so I try to ask her to come over as much as possible.

"I know what we can toast to," I hear Ash say.

"What?" I ask.

"That!" She pokes me in the arm. "Look before he disappears!"

I turn my head. And then I hear her refilling my glass, but I don't see her doing it. Because my eyes are transfixed by what's coming up over the hill.

It's a runner. That's not unusual in this neighborhood. I live close to Reed's Lake, and there's a 4.5 mile trail that wraps around it. We get bikers, runners, people with strollers, and more dogs than you can count.

But as the morning sun highlights this young, firm jogger, I gasp a little and then, much to my dismay, I actually say "Hubba hubba."

Brynn snort-laughs and sprays orange juice everywhere, but Ash just sighs.

The man really is breathtaking. He's the perfect specimen—broad shoulders, a chest that's lean and chiseled, rippling with motion. He's wearing these tiny yellow running shorts that I'm just hoping show off what must be a fine ass as he passes us. But first it's the V that gets me. You know, that V of muscle from the ribs to the hips, that surely must lead to something I just want to wrap my mouth around and...

He's getting closer. Why is he slowing down?

"Please show a little of your ass," I whisper. I don't mean to say it out loud, but if you really want something, saying it out loud helps make it happen, right?

Brynn, Ash, and I are completely frozen, staring at this luscious man running past.

Only he doesn't run past.

What is he doing? Why is he running up the lawn? Why is he stopping in front of my house and waving his hand.

And then I figure it out. This hunk of man, this specimen of perfection, this young god—knows me.

It's Liam! My girls' babysitter. The kid I used to babysit. And all I want to do is hump him. Right here, right now. As I gaze upon his beautiful body, the urge is staggering. My hormones are rising into the air around me like a mist.

No! No no no no! Thou shalt not perve on the younger man! Shut up, hormones! Oh, hell. I'm a cougar.

Panicking, I look at Brynn and Ash. "Gahhhh," I manage.

They'll understand, right? Surely they'll step in and save the day? I mean—that's what best friends are for, yes?

"This is gonna be good," Brynn says. Ash laughs.

Bitches.

"Hi," I squeak.

"Hi," he says. "This your place?"

Liam's sweat-shined chest is rising and falling as he pants from the heat. I'm staring at it. "What was the question?"

There are giggles from the peanut gallery.

"Your house, Sadie?" he says, glancing up at it. "Do you live here?"

"Yup, yup, uh-huh," I babble.

Liam leans forward and peers into my empty glass. "I think that mimosa has gone to your brain."

"I think so too!" I say, leaping at this excuse for both my flapping tongue and my wandering eyes. "I have no tolerance anymore."

"Mimosa for you, too, sir?" Ash offers brightly. "If you drink one, you'll be saving Sadie from having a hangover. I'm Ash, by the way. And our friend here is Brynn. She didn't swallow a beach ball, she's pregnant."

"I got that," Liam says, watching Ash pour a drink. "That's for me? But I'm in the middle of a run."

"You're taking an intermission," she says. "Juice is healthy." Weirdly, he seems to accept this. Ash has that effect on people. He takes the glass from her hand and smiles at me.

And that smile makes my vaginal muscles contract ever so slightly. What is *wrong* with me?

Goddammit. Liam reclines his gleaming body against the porch pillar, and it's an effort not to swallow my tongue. It feels so wrong to be so attracted to Liam. When I babysat for his parents, he was just a pimply teenager.

I can't deny the effect he has on me, though. Every day at pickup time when I thank him for taking good care of my girls, I find myself blushing. A good psychologist knows all the physical signs of attraction—the rapid breathing, the sweaty hands. The dilated pupils and the southern blood flow.

At the moment I'm experiencing all these at once. For Liam.

I am obviously a horrible person.

Liam watches me over the rim of his glass as he takes a sip. "Mmm. Thank you." He sits his glorious body down on my front stoop. "Where are my favorite two-year-olds today?"

"At their father's house," I say. And then I feel it—the slap of

13

shame that always hits me when I admit that I'm divorced. Half the time I feel like I'm wearing a sandwich board. *My husband left me for a younger woman.* As if anyone who looks at me will be able to see it.

But Liam absorbs this information with a beaming smile. "You're single?"

Even though I refuse to glance at my friends, I can feel their ears perking up at the tone of his question.

"Divorced," I mumble. *My husband wasn't attracted to me anymore.* It still hurts. I don't think it will ever stop.

"Where do you two know each other from?" Brynn asks.

"Now there's a story," I say, letting out a nervous laugh.

"Sadie was our babysitter," Liam says, leaning his head against the porch rail. He looks like a lazy cat. "I was fourteen and desperately in love with her."

There is an audible gasp from Brynn and Ash.

"I know!" Liam grins. "Hot for the babysitter. Such a clichè. But can you blame me? Sadie is everything. She's cute and super smart. I had really good taste even when I was in eighth grade."

Brynn and Ash sigh.

"What are you ladies doing this fine morning?" he asks, sipping his drink.

"This," Ash says. "Drinking our breakfast and trying to get Sadie to sign up for Tinder."

His blue eyes lift to mine. "Thinking of dating again?"

"It's too soon," I stammer. "The best I can manage is coffee with a guy named Earl."

"Dinner," Ash corrects. "You're going to dinner with him like a big girl."

"It's a bad idea," I insist. Now that Liam is sitting here, it sounds like a worse idea than it did a half hour ago. I've obviously been off the market for too long. Men have a strange effect on me now. Case in point: I was practically drooling all over myself when Liam ran up the walkway.

"Nah, it's a great idea," Liam says. "Doesn't have to be a life-changing evening. But just showing up for one date takes some of the mystique away."

"It breaks the seal," Brynn add.

"It pops your cherry," Ash puts in.

"Let's not get carried away," I mutter. Coffee is scary. Dinner is terrifying. But the idea of showing a stranger my post-childbirth naked body is all the way into horror movie territory. I doubt I could do it.

"Did you do your Tinder profile yet?" Liam wonders.

"Not really," I sigh. "I don't know what to say."

"Oh, please." Liam makes an impatient noise. "First you take a photo. Just wear that red top with the..." He waves a hand to indicate the flowing sleeves of my gypsy blouse that I was wearing yesterday when I picked up the girls. "That says *playful and feminine* but it doesn't say, *here is my cleavage*."

"Good pick!" Ash agrees. "Sadie looks dreamy in that."

"It's very Sadie," Liam agrees, as if he's known me all my life.

And he has, I guess. Our families went to the same church. But I'm still experiencing cognitive dissonance when I look at this hot, muscular stranger. Intellectually I know the old Liam is in there somewhere. But it just doesn't quite seem real.

"What should her profile say?" Ash asks pointedly. "We want to weed out the losers."

"Oh, that's easy. Let 'em know right away that Sadie is smarter than they are. Anyone who's intimidated can fuck right off," Liam says. He rests a hand casually on his six-pack, and for some reason my mouth is watering.

"She can't post her IQ, though," Ash snorts. "So how do we get that across?"

"Simple," he insists. "Hot young MILF with a graduate degree and awesome friends seeks smart man with good teeth. Interest in scary movies a plus. Boom. Done."

"Good teeth?" I squeak. "Why add that?"

"It's a code," Liam says, nodding like a sage. "It's hard to have your life together and not have good teeth."

The things I don't know about online dating. And then I squint, because how does he know I like horror? "And the scary movies?"

"You don't *remember*?" he asks, clutching his chest like I've wounded him. "That summer you babysat me and you let me stay up and we watched *The Shining*. It was a turning point in my life. Then we moved on to Hitchcock, and you gave me a thorough education."

And suddenly I do remember. "We watched all the classics," I say slowly. It was really fun, too. Up until then I did all my scary-movie watching solo. But Liam was eager to be initiated into the joys of on-screen terror. "You liked *The Birds* more than *Vertigo*."

"Still do!"

Those were the days when summer seemed a million years long. And I never felt lonely.

"We had the *best* time," he says. "Without your introduction, I wouldn't have seen *It Follows*, or *The Babadook*..."

I let out a little shriek of excitement. "You've seen *Get Out*, right?"

"Obvs," Liam says, and now we're grinning at each other. "I can't wait for his new one."

Ash clears her throat, and when I glance at her she's wearing an evil little smile. That's never good. I make a note to figure out why later. "Okay, scary movies are a good addition to my profile," I say. "*If* I make a profile."

"Where's your phone?" Ash demands of me. "Let's make it right now!"

"No way," I say loud enough to prevent argument. "I never agreed to Tinder. I agreed to one date. To break the seal or whatever we're calling it. Dating again is like getting into a cold swimming pool. I have to inch my way in with tiny little trial splashes to my skin."

"I always just dive into the deep end," Liam says. "Works great." He gives me a wink, and I swear my friends nearly topple into their drinks.

"You live in the neighborhood?" Brynn asks. She's trying to sound nonchalant, but I can hear all the things she and Ash aren't saying. *This stud lives in your neighborhood. You can be fuck buddies!*

"Yeah. One street over." He points vaguely in the direction of my backyard.

"Really?" I ask. "Did your family move?"

Liam laughs. "No? But I did. They're still knocking around the same place over on Wilshire. Cassidy is living with them just for the summer, until her fellowship at Oxford starts up."

"Cassidy has a fellowship at Oxford?" I'm still picturing a nine-year-old with pigtails.

"Her subject is applied mathematics for crime prediction and criminal law."

"*Applied* mathematics," Brynn echoes slowly. "My subject is applied sauces and dips. I apply them to food and then put them in my mouth."

"Well, you're eating for two," Liam says, gulping his drink.

"Nope. That's pretty much all the time." Brynn looks around. "When can we eat again? Does now work for you guys?"

"But we just ate!" I complain.

Chuckling, Liam gets to his feet. "I like the way you girls party. Thanks for the pick-me-up," he says, handing Ash his glass. "I have to finish my seven miles. See you Monday, Sadie!"

Liam gives us a wave and jogs down my front walk.

We all watch his ass as he goes. I think I let out a little whimper of confusion. I shouldn't perve on Liam. Those buns, though...

"Well!" Ash hisses when he's out of sight. "Why didn't you tell us about him?

"What about him? I hadn't seen him in fifteen years until I dropped the girls off at daycare. We were never close."

"Clearly you need to be closer," Brynn points out. "Skin to skin, maybe."

"Stop it, you guys. He's too young for me."

"How old is he?" Ash asks.

I do the math. "Twenty-nine, I guess."

"Omigod!" Brynn squeaks. "He's practically jailbait."

"Right?" I agree.

Ash smacks me in the back of the head. "She was *kidding*."

"Oh. But still. So what? I'm sure he has a swarm of single twenty-something women in his life, who are primed and ready to..."

"...Hone his bone," Ash puts in.

"Doesn't matter," Brynn insists. "Did you hear him? He totally wants Sadie."

"No, he doesn't!" I yelp. "Please."

My friends' heads swivel, and they give me matching looks of disdain. "Girl, you're the shrink. You're supposed to be able to read people," Brynn complains.

"He called you a hot MILF," Ash says.

"He noticed your red gypsy blouse," Brynn adds.

"He was *desperately in love* with you!" Ash cries. "That's a direct quote."

"He wants to put ranch dressing on your Hidden Valley," Brynn offers.

There's a pause and then all of us, including Brynn, say "ewwwww."

Brynn shrugs. "Sorry. I think about food all the time. I can't help it."

"Bottom line," Ash says. "You have to hit that. Forget Earl."

"I'm not hitting anything," I repeat. It's too terrifying. I know my limits. "And Liam was just being nice. That's what he is. He's nice. A nice boy."

"Boy toy, maybe," Ash says with a smirk.

I ignore her. It's best to ignore Ash when she says something that's a little too truthful.

I take a big drink of my third mimosa, because I could really use a boy toy in my life. Or at least in my bed.

3 WHINE O'CLOCK

Liam

A FEW DAYS later I'm at work at the daycare. It's ten after five, and the last of the kids in my care are starting to sag. It's whine o'clock in the toddler room.

"Blade," I say to a little boy who's brandishing two wooden blocks like weapons. "Please put those back in the block box. Your dad will be here any minute."

He gives me a sullen face but then ambles toward the blocks. Blade is a good kid most of the time, in spite of his unfortunate name. He's a very ambitious nose-picker, but nobody is perfect. And I grudgingly admire his dedication to the craft.

I cross the room and pluck Sadie's daughter Kate off the roof of the playhouse. Again. "Too high up," I explain. "It will hurt when you fall."

"Boosht," she says. It's her favorite word. I'm pretty sure she means *bullshit*, but I don't call her on it. You have to pick your battles. "Hi," Kate says in my arms. But she isn't talking to me. She's talking to her twin sister, who I've been wearing like a cape for the past twenty minutes. Amy gets cuddly when she's tired.

"Mama coming?" Amy asks.

A glance at the door reveals Sadie just walking into the reception area, wearing a killer short skirt and a slightly frazzled expression. She told me her last appointment of the day always ends at four-thirty, and then she sprints here to pick up the girls, so they don't have to stay even one minute extra.

"I don't know," I tell the girls. "Who is that pretty lady over there?"

There is an instant shriek. In stereo. Sadie spots us from the doorway and her face softens. The girls are wiggling, so I kneel down to unload them. Sadie unlatches the half-door that prevents escape from the two-year-old room and makes it about three paces in before she's swarmed.

"Hello!" she coos. "I missed you so much!"

Kate starts up a monologue right away, unloading the days triumphs and miseries. But Amy just snuggles in close to her mother's bosom.

Lucky kid. My appreciation for Sadie's curves is entirely different than Amy's, but no less strong. It's fair to say that Sadie was my first real crush. In fact, I'm pretty sure that Sadie is the entire reason that I tend to date older women.

Sadie and I spent a lot of time together the summer before I turned fifteen. She was a twenty-year-old college student, employed by my parents to take care of my siblings.

At first I'd protested my parents hiring a babysitter since I was clearly old enough and wise enough to be on my own. I remember my mom trying to convince me that the babysitter wasn't for me but for Connor, Aiden, and Cassidy who were eleven, nine, and seven years old.

As soon as Sadie walked in the door, wearing a tank top, cut-off jeans, and huge glasses, with her brown hair falling to the rise of her breasts, I immediately stopped complaining. I knew a good thing when I saw it, and that good thing was Sadie.

And I wasn't wrong. Not only was Sadie hot, she was also kind to me. We had long conversations while the younger ones played. They were the kids, at least in my mind. And in spite of my young age I thought of myself as Sadie's equal, and therefore a serious contender for Sadie's heart.

Those movies we watched together were some of the most fun I'd ever had. I'd ride my bike to Blockbuster and rent titles from the horror section, because Sadie always became happy and animated when we discussed them. She'd choose one, and then we'd sit out on the screened porch with a little TV I'd carried out there for exactly this purpose.

Best summer ever. She'd squeak at the jump scares and sometimes grab my wrist. And I'd sit there trying to be manly and not crap myself when the movie came to its terrifying climax.

When the film was done, we'd shut off the TV and laugh about how scared we'd been. Or we'd make fun of the parts that didn't work very well.

And then I'd go to bed and lay awake thinking about how much I needed to hold her, and how it would feel to kiss her. It's kind of a miracle that I never tried to make a move on her. And thank God I didn't. The disappointment would have been mortifying.

Sadie always took me seriously, never condescended to me, and then on the last day of her employment, she took my breath away. "Thanks for all the help this summer. You're going to grow up to be an amazing person." And then she kissed me. On the lips.

Okay, no. It was really on the cheek. But it didn't feel harmless and platonic to me. That chaste kiss fueled hours upon hours of brand new Sadie Mathews fantasies afterward.

I still remember the softness of her lips.

And now I realize she's standing right in front of me, talking to me, and I somehow missed it.

"Liam? Are you okay?"

Yep. Just thinking about how much I want to own your mouth, for real this time. "Yep. Sure. Okey-dokey," I stammer. And I want to die. For real.

"I'm ready to relieve you of your burden," she says and I honestly have no idea what she's talking about. Then she points to my back and I see that I'm wearing Amy again. How did that happen? I don't remember reaching for her.

Wait a minute, fourteen-year-old Liam asks. *Was there a moment when we were close to Sadie's breasts and didn't realize it?*

Funny thing—I hadn't heard from teenage Liam for years, but he speaks up whenever Sadie walks into the room, usually to whisper filthy desires in my ear.

Fourteen-year-old Liam is not very smooth.

"Oh! Sorry!" I peel Amy off of me and transfer her into Sadie's warm, waiting arms. At least I think they're warm. God, they must be warm. And velvety.

Focus, Liam!

"I just wanted to say..." Sadie starts and I'm a little breathless again. Is she going to say she wants to get together? Because I'm up for that. Dinner. A movie. Laving my tongue all over her body...once the twins are fast asleep of course. But she doesn't tell me what she wanted to say because her cell rings. She holds up a finger in a "just a sec" way and takes a couple of steps away, but I can still hear her hushed conversation. Or at least her side of it.

"Yes, Decker, I can hear you fine." Pause. "What? You've got to be kidding me! Decker...this is the third time you've cancelled." Pause. "Well maybe I have plans too." Pause. "I *do* have plans. I have a life. Actually, I have a date tonight." Pause. "No. I *can't* ask Brynn to watch them. She's eight months pregnant. And don't even mention Ash—the last time she watched them, they set her on fire." Pause. "Yes. It was a small fire, but still. There was smoke." Pause. "Gosh, I guess I'll cancel my plans because your plans are obviously more important." Pause. "*Thank you?* Seriously? Can you not tell when I'm using irony..." Then she looks down at the phone. "Unbelievable! He just hung up on me!"

"Who's dat?" Kate asks.

"Oh, um, nobody, sweetie. Mommy's just rearranging things. Instead of going to daddy's tonight for movies, I thought you'd stay with me and we'd watch movies at home!"

Her false cheerfulness makes me wince. Before I really think it through, I hear myself say, "Actually, I could watch the girls for you tonight."

Sadie opens her mouth to reply, and I'm certain she's about to tell me what a terrible idea that is when all of a sudden the girls erupt with happiness. They're screaming "Liam! Liam! Liam!" in unison.

Twin Brain. It's a thing.

But that was a real rookie move on my part. I know better than to offer something like that before I know whether Sadie would say yes. Now I've got her girls all riled up.

"Liam, I couldn't ask that of you," she says, but her body language isn't sure. I can tell. In fact, I've always been able to read Sadie. And she wants to ask me, but she feels shy.

"It's no problem. Really. I don't have plans," I lie.

"It's Friday night. And you're...single?"

I nod.

"And you don't have plans?"

"Nope." It's a good thing I'm not hooked up to a lie detector right now, because I was going to meet my brothers at a bar. There was some promise of them setting me up with someone, but I can totally cancel that. Because I'd rather spend the night with Sadie.

I mentally face-palm, because I *won't* be spending the night with Sadie. I'll be spending the night with Sadie's girls while Sadie goes out with some douchebag who I just know doesn't deserve her and probably has an erectile issue. Hopefully.

I have no such issue.

"Really, I'm happy to do it. Give me, what, an hour to go home and shower and I'll come over and you can...do...what you need to do." I have to speak up because Kate is screaming "Yeah Yeah Yeah!" and Amy is sucking so joyously on her pacifier that I'm afraid she's going to create a black hole.

"That would be..." she thinks about it.

God, she smells good when she's thinking, fourteen-year-old Liam says.

"...Really amazing," she says with a sigh. "Thank you! I can pay you, of course."

"Please. Don't worry about it. You can owe me." I'm thinking of the many ways she could repay me but then realize I might come off as creepy. "A beer."

"I can do that," she says. "A beer."

And some dry humping. Please, God, some dry humping, the four-teen-year-old in me says. Thank God I don't say that aloud. Instead I say "Cool. Coolio. Cool."

And I want to die all over again. It feels like I'll always be a teenager around Sadie. Thankfully, she doesn't comment and just smiles.

———

An hour later I'm standing on Sadie's porch, still feeling awkward. She'll always have that effect on me—like I don't belong in this body. I should be holding something, like a bottle of wine or a bouquet of flowers. Instead, I've got a backpack stuffed with educational games, and I've loaded my phone with the greatest musical hits for toddlers. It's not, thankfully, things like the Wiggles. This is a list I've curated myself. Education starts early and they need to learn what real music is.

I knock again, and just as I'm starting to wonder if she's changed her mind, the door swings open and...holy shit. *Hello, goddess.* Her long hair falls around her shoulders in natural curls. She's wearing a filmy sundress and strappy heels and I swear to

God, with the light behind her, I can see the outline of all of her curves. I'm pretty sure I gulp audibly.

"Liam! My hero!" she cries and then she's hugging me. She smells like flowers. She smells like moonlight and secrets and wishes.

The hug lasts only a second. I want to string it out the way you can make taffy longer by pulling on it.

"Come in!" she says, beckoning.

I follow her inside to find that her home is just as I imagined. It's like walking into a warm embrace. Dark wood floors, open spaces, a grey couch, and two deep-green velvet chairs. There are pillows everywhere. It's a lot of fucking pillows, but I'm good with that. Pillows can be really useful.

Especially during sex, my fourteen-year-old self whispers.

"I'm running late! Just come in and make yourself at home."

I step in further. I hear Amy before I see her. Her pacifier works like a bell on a cat's collar. "Up!" she slurps. I set my bag down and scoop her up. "Liam!" she says, somehow still sucking her pacifier.

"I really don't think I'll be gone long," I hear Sadie calling out to me and I catch a glimpse of her in the bathroom. She's debating between lipstick shades. She should just keep her lips bare. So much more kissable.

"Try the red one," I suggest. It'll look good with her dress and also maybe work to deter the guy she's seeing from trying to make a move on her.

"Right," she says, sort of breathless, and then she slides the color over her lips and makes an air kiss. I turn away because I just can't look at her doing that. I'm here to help out. Nothing more. I'm just the babysitter.

"Ready," Amy says. "She's running." I'm a little confused by what she means and then I hear Kate. She's wearing her helmet and approaching at top speed. I brace myself as she barrels into me full force.

"Oof," I say. For real. I mean, there's the makings of a football player in her. I should introduce her to my brother Aiden. Maybe he could coach her.

Suddenly I've got my hands full of two squirming kiddos. They're adorable. It's like trying to hold onto water.

"Mama looks weird," Kate says.

"I do?" Sadie's expression is horrified.

"You mean Mama looks perfect," I suggest.

"'Kay. She looks perfect weird."

"I hope it's just the lipstick. They're not used to seeing me dress up." She takes a final look at herself and says, "Well, I guess this is as good as it gets."

That's curious to me. She looks incredible. But then Sadie has always looked incredible. There's something about her spirit that just sort of shines through.

And there I go again.

I need to get laid.

Maybe Sadie'd be up for that?

I shake my head. *Babysitter. I'm the babysitter.*

I turn my focus from Sadie to the girls. "What should we do first? Playdough or Herbs and Flowers?"

"Herbs and Flowers?" Sadie asks.

"It's a matching game. It teaches them some of our local flora. Morels. Trillium. Ladyslippers."

She looks at me and I can't quite read her expression. "Oh. Great. Okay. Good. So I'll..."

"You'll head out?" I ask.

"Yes. Uhm...they've eaten. Kate has a tiny..."

"Ear infection. I know. She needs to finish her antibiotics. And Amy is probably due for a snack in an hour. Bedtime at 8?"

Again, there's that curious look. "Yes. Exactly." It's quiet for a second. Then both Kate and Amy with their Twin Brain say "Go!"

"Looks like they want to spend some time with you," she says.

"Movie!" Amy says.

Before Sadie can tell me what they want to watch, I've already opened my bag and pulled out a stack of DVDs. "I've got this," I say. "Go have fun. Go crazy."

What I want to say is, *ditch that dude and stay here with me. At 8:01 we can play our own kind of game.*

But it's not to be. Sadie's always been my fantasy, and that's all she'll ever be. Half the time she still looks at me like I'm fourteen, and I'm not sure how to get her past that.

"Thanks a bunch," she says.

"Is he picking you up?" I ask.

"Who?"

"Your date."

"Earl? Oh. No. He suggested we meet at the restaurant. It's closer to his house and...I don't know. I'll get a Lyft so I can have a drink with dinner guilt-free."

He's not picking her up? I firmly believe this guy is a dick.

She checks her phone. "Ah. I guess the car is here. I'll just go."

She kisses the girls one by one. I wish she'd kiss me, too. *Come on, Sadie, my body is ready!*

I grab the door for her. "If you need anything," I say, "Anything at all, I'm here." And I mean it.

She nods and then runs off to her Lyft.

"Herbs and Flowers and then movie time!" I say excitedly, hoping the girls can't sense the disappointment in my voice.

4 EARL. JUST EARL.

Sadie

"SHE'LL HAVE the citrus chicken salad," Earl says, sealing his fate as the wrong man for me. "I'll have the steak au poivre, a loaded baked potato, and the broccoli."

"Yessir," our young waiter says, as if ordering for another adult is a normal thing to do. "What would the lady like to drink?"

"White wine," Earl says.

"No!" I practically shout, just so I don't miss the chance to take my destiny into my own hands. A couple of heads swivel in our direction, but it can't be helped. "I'll have the..." My mind goes blank. Because, dammit, white wine is my go-to beverage. The waiter points to the drink menu on the table and I pronounce the first thing I see. "A red-headed slut," I say.

"Coming right up," the waiter says before running away.

Whoops. That probably sends the wrong message. But there's cranberry in it and I adore cranberry.

"I like your style," Earl says, leaning back in his chair. He's wearing a T-shirt with a wolf and the American flag flapping in the background. I don't know what message it's trying to send, but I feel like it's a clue.

"My *style*," I say frostily, "is to order for myself." How has this man managed to piss me off at the four-minute mark of our date? I didn't even agree to dinner. Only drinks.

"You seem like the citrus chicken salad type," he says with a shrug.

"Oh, really? You can tell that just from looking at me?" And— goddammit. I *am* the citrus chicken salad type. But that doesn't make it right.

He lifts a shoulder in a halfhearted shrug. He's not unattractive. He's got taut forearms and a tanned face that has a certain manly appeal. If he weren't a giant, gaping asshole then maybe I would enjoy the view.

I can't believe I put on lipstick and a dress for this misogynistic prick.

"Where do you work?" I ask him, just hoping to find a safe topic of conversation.

"I have my own accounting firm."

"Oh!" That's encouraging. A nice, safe job. "Who are your clients, primarily?"

"Militias."

"Mil...what?"

"Independent militia groups. We believe that many federal regulations are unlawful. That the federal government has seized liberty from the people. It's time to stand up and take them back. The Sovereign Citizens Movement aims to put power back in the hands of the righteous."

"O-kayyy," I say slowly. I should probably be afraid. But we're in the middle of a busy restaurant, and I'll admit that I'm fascinated. I am, after all, a shrink. And most of the patients seeking treatment in my office aren't as colorful. "So how *does* an accountant assist a militia?"

"Well, we don't believe in federal taxation."

I let out a nervous giggle. "That must make your job easier, right? Less to do before April fifteenth?"

"Oh, no ma'am." He shakes his head. "I'm a very busy man all year long. Opening shell corporations and offshore accounts takes up a lot of time."

Right. Of course it does. Maybe he's kidding though. I take a good, long look at him.

I don't think he's kidding. His American flag waves at me.

"Cabernet for the gentleman," our waiter says. "One red-headed slut for the lady."

"Thank you," I say with the best smile I can muster. Then I pick up the glass and drink half of it immediately.

———

"Oh dear," I say about forty minutes later to Mirror Sadie. I'm staring at my reflection in the women's bathroom. My lipstick is all chewed off.

And that's not even my biggest problem.

I'm wasted. Or *pissed*, as they say in Britain. "I got pissed, because I was pissed off," I tell Mirror Sadie.

A woman washing her hands a few feet away gives me a funny look.

"Bad date," I say, but I slur it a little. I sound like there are marbles in my mouth. Maybe there are.

Note to shelf! No—self. *Whatever*. Note to Sadie! Eat more than the citrus chicken salad if you're going to drink three red-headed sluts in a row. I don't know what's in them, but I've discovered that cranberry is not the only ingredient.

Although I think it stained my tongue. I stick my tongue out and examine it. "Dah mah tongue wook weed?" I ask Mirror Sadie.

The other woman washing her hands flees. She doesn't even dry.

It's difficult to see my tongue in this light, so I take my phone out of my purse and take a selfie. Of my tongue. There should be a word for that.

Oh wait—there is. It's called *stalling*. I'm taking photos of my tongue so I don't have to see Earl's stupid face.

A text pings on my phone.

Yay! A text! More stalling! I see that it's from Liam. A less drunk woman would probably think, *Oh dear, are the girls okay?* But my first reaction is a quivering in my lady parts.

Also, it's a photo text. If there were something wrong I wouldn't get a picture of Liam on the sofa with my girls snuggled up to either side of him. There's a bowl of popcorn in his lap, and they all look gloriously happy.

This is your proof of life photo, he writes. **Enjoy your date and don't worry about a thing**.

I just stare at the picture a little longer. The truth is I'm not at all afraid to leave my girls with Liam. That guy just exudes the sort of confidence that toddlers respond to. He's like a stone in the river—no matter how much chaos surges around him, it doesn't budge him. He's our rock. Rock hard...

Uh-oh. I realize I'm staring at Liam instead of at my children. That six-pack, though. You can see the ripples beneath his polo shirt.

The women's restroom door opens to admit three laughing women, and suddenly the place is crowded. With great reluctance I leave the peaceful seclusion of the bathroom and slowly walk back toward our table. If I'm lucky, Earl gave up on me and went home.

No such luck. He's still there, and he's eating a piece of cherry pie.

There is no dessert in front of my place. "Where's mine?" I demand, because his bad behavior has infected me like a virus.

"You didn't like me ordering for you," he says. Then he finishes the pie in two bites.

The young waiter approaches the table. "Would you like any dessert?" he asks, eyeing the empty pie plate with a disapproving frown.

"Just the check," I grumble. "And quickly."

"Right away, ma'am," he says before disappearing.

"I've been ma'amed," I complain.

"What should he have called you?" Earl asks, licking the fork. Then he turns it over and licks the other side. *Ew.*

"It never hurts to hear *miss*," I inform him. The *ma'am* thing started happening about two seconds after Decker told me I have an unattractive mom bod. One day I was "miss" and the next day, "ma'am."

"Can I drive you home, *miss?*" Earl asks, a dirty gleam in his eye.

"Yes, please," I say. I don't want to pay for another Lyft. And I'm not entirely confident I would type in my home address right now. Not accurately.

The waiter returns with the check. I glare at Earl until he throws down his credit card. And, lookee here! The waiter has also brought me a fresh red-headed slut. He probably feels sorry for me. I pick that sucker up and drain it. This night can't end soon enough.

5 WHAT HAPPENS AFTER TOO MANY RED-HEADED SLUTS

Liam

THIS NIGHT CAN'T END SOON ENOUGH. These toddlers are tired, but they won't fall asleep.

"Liam!" I hear for the hundredth time.

"I'm right here," I call through their bedroom door. I've left it open just a crack. I'm sitting in the carpeted hallway outside their room, so they won't be tempted to climb out of their cribs to come and find me.

Again.

"It's quiet time, now," I say calmly. "You don't have to sleep, but you must close your eyes and think about it."

"Okay," Kate's sleepy voice says.

"Piggypoo?" Amy asks.

"You have him," I say, not budging. She wants me to check on her again.

Sadie's twins are so stinking cute. I love to watch their little minds at work. After we watched the video I brought them —*Elmo Meets the Wild Horses*—they had to *play* horses. That's how

34

toddlers make sense of the things they see and hear. They reenact them.

It hadn't occurred to me that I would be the horse in this scenario, however. My knees will never be the same. Live and learn.

It gets quiet in the girls' room, and I let myself relax. I'm bone-tired. Every day I spend ten hours with toddlers. A few more shouldn't matter, right? After work I'll often lift weights and take a seven mile run. I'm a high-energy kind of guy.

But about an hour ago, my get-up-and-go just got up and went. Soon I'll be off duty, so it doesn't really matter. I can go home and open a beer and think of nothing but my weekend plans and myself.

As I sit here outside the kids' room, I realize that Sadie is never off the clock. Even when I'm watching her kids, she's still the mom. I'm sure she loves it. I'm sure she loves *them*. But I'll bet it's emotionally exhausting.

And Monday, when I go back to work, I'll have a new appreciation for the tired adults at pickup time, straggling in and pasting on excited faces when their exhausted children launch themselves into overworked arms.

I hear a sudden thump. And then a bump. *Uh-oh!* I strain my ears, listening for activity on the other side of the girls' door.

But a moment later it becomes clear that the sounds I'm hearing aren't coming from the twins' room, but from the front door. I get up and sprint downstairs to find Sadie just pushing open the door, her expression dazed.

"You got it now," a guy's voice says. Then he chuckles. "You're a fun drunk, honey." When the guy—I think his name is Earl—comes into view behind Sadie, his hand is on her hip.

The urge to slap his mitts away from her body is so strong that I have to shove my own hands in my pockets to prevent myself from doing it. "Hey there, Sadie." I'm using my Calm Voice—the one I employ when a toddler is just about to explode in tears. I stretch out a hand to Sadie and she takes it, her smooth fingers closing around mine.

"Let's get you into bed," Earl says.

"No way," I bark.

The dude's eyes widen. "And who are you?"

"An old friend," I say through gritted teeth. "I got this, okay?" It's possible Earl isn't trying to take advantage of Sadie. She obviously needs to find a flat surface. Pronto. Her eyes are glassy and I've seen steadier walking in the infants' room at the daycare.

"Go. Thanks," Sadie slurs over her shoulder. "I'm good."

The guy rolls his eyes. "Why do women always get wasted when they're out with me?"

"Because you're a misogynist?" Sadie mumbles.

His expression darkens. "*What* did you call me? Is that how you thank a man for dinner?"

Sadie doesn't answer. Then the man calls out, "I'm not even attracted to you! You talk and think too much!"

A split second later I've pulled Sadie behind my body and I'm up in this guy's face. "Time to go home," I say through gritted teeth.

"She's all yours. She costs a fortune in drinks," he says, giving me an evil smile.

"Back off," I hiss.

He scowls at me, and I consider the possibility that he's about to sucker-punch me. But then he turns around and marches out the door and off the front porch.

Behind me, Sadie heaves a huge sigh of relief.

"That bad, huh?" I ask, feeling relieved, too.

"Terrible!" she yelps. "He ordered for me. A salad. At a steak place."

"What?" I turn around and take a good look at her. And, damn. She's so freaking beautiful. Those full lips and wavy hair used to appear regularly in my fantasies. Who am I kidding? They still do. Fourteen-year-old Liam is panting at the sight of Sadie's cleavage and those tan legs.

How could that douche not be attracted to her? Of course he was attracted to her. He just said that to soothe his ego. I seriously want to carry her up the stairs and peel that dress off her luscious body.

"He ordered for me! And he admitted to me that he sued his own mother." She shakes her head, incredulous. "Four red-headed sluts later..." She shrugs her shoulders.

None of that makes any sense, but she's doing her best. I take one of her smooth hands in mine and gently lead her toward the living room. "Come on, now. Have a seat." I sort of pour her onto the couch. "Take those shoes off."

She obeys with much less pushback than I get from the two-year-old set at work. Taking care of toddlers and drunk people demands similar skills.

"How are K-kamy?" She blinks. "Kate and Amy."

"Asleep," I assure her, sitting down beside her. "We watched a video about wild ponies and read some horrible book about a Sparkle Princess."

Sadie laughs suddenly, low and throaty. The sound goes straight to my balls. "Worst book *ever*. Sometimes that book gets 'lost' on the top shelf in my closet."

"You bad girl," I whisper, teasing her. "You should get a spanking." *Whoops.* I guess fourteen-year-old Liam added that last bit. He's kind of an asshole.

Sadie doesn't call me on my overtly inappropriate suggestion. Her eyes widen, though. And then her drunk gaze makes a slow tour of my body. She starts with my mouth. I watch her examining my lips as she parts her own.

I lick mine, just to see what she'll do.

She takes a sharp breath, and then her eyes continue their journey, down my chest, until they look pointedly at my lap.

And then she sighs. "I should go to sleep."

"Yes, you should," I cheerfully agree. I'm suddenly in a perfect mood. Sadie Mathews just checked me out. She's done it before, too. Her eyes were practically stapled to my bare chest that day I discovered her on the porch with her friends.

I get checked out all the time, because I am a very fine specimen. But if Sadie Mathews is checking me out, that's a good day."Come on," I say. "It's beddie time."

I help her stand up and she sort of falls against me. She fits perfectly. "I don't want beddie time." She pouts. "I want..."

And then she's got her hands on my chest. I think she's trying to push away so I let go, but no. She starts at my neck and then runs the palms of her hands down my torso. Do I tighten my core just a little so my chest is rock hard? Hell yes. I haven't spent all those hours in the gym for naught. I have prepared for this moment.

"Jesus Christ," she whispers. Her hands have stopped on my abs. "I could play patty cake with your chest." I'm not sure what she means, exactly, but she's sort of slapping my chest, and I'm okay with that.

She's tempting. So. Tempting.

But I am a gentleman. With dirty, dirty thoughts. But still a gentleman.

————

Sadie

Apparently four red-headed sluts is the magic number to disconnect my intellect from my impulses. How else can I explain standing here in Liam's arms with my palms against his chest? Meanwhile, my inner red-headed slut whispers, *Take it off. Take off your shirt. Your shirt. Just take it. Off.*

I can picture myself rubbing my hands all over his body. Unbuckling his belt and pulling down his pants, stripping him right here in front of me. Maybe I fall to my knees in worship. Or maybe he falls to his.

My brain and my body are only intermittently communicating. So I suddenly blurt: "I haven't had sex in a year!" Then I gasp because I just admitted that. But do I shut up now? Nooo. "Actually," I babble, "it's closer to two years, but only if you count that one time when I was trying to convince myself that Decker still loved me and so I accidentally had sex with him."

There's a pause. I can hear the ticking of the clock and the static from the baby monitors. "Accidentally?" asks Liam. "Did you fall on his dick?"

And I laugh, which is also a problem. I have, uh, a rather peculiar laugh that I try to conceal, because it's low. Really low. It's— fuck it. I have a man-laugh, okay? So I'm man-laughing right now. Standing in my living room, my hands roaming all over the babysitter, I man-laugh at the image of me accidentally sliding on a banana peel, tumbling, and falling onto my ex-husband's dick.

Then, suddenly it's not funny anymore. Because after that episode, Decker ended up telling me he'd accidentally had sex with our nanny. And that he'd accidentally fallen in love with her.

"It's not my fault," he'd said. "It was an accident."

All the drunken joy drains out of me. I hate my life.

If I'm honest, that last time with Decker was entirely forgettable, too. Accident or not. "I'm not going to count that time, actually," I decide aloud. Because I am brilliant. I have the power to choose the way I view things.

And I'm drunk. Drunk drunky drunk.

"So you haven't had sex in *two* years?" Liam gapes at me. I've blown his mind.

"I know! Two! And if we're only counting *good* sex, it's even longer. Dinosaurs roamed the earth when I last had dirty, sweaty, clawing-at-each-other sex."

Liam swallows audibly. "I could help you with that," he offers. "I specialize in good sex. The sweaty kind."

We just blink at each other for a second.

"...I mean, I've had a crush on you since I was fourteen and we spent that summer..." He clears his throat before continuing to cover up that cute little crack in his voice. Puberty all over again. "That summer we spent together." His voice is much lower this time.

Now my mind is blown. There's a peculiar energy vibrating through me. And I'm actually considering stripping naked right here. Where's a banana peel when I need one? Then I could—oops!—accidentally have sex with this young, hot stud. Fall right on his dick. And I'll bet it's a really nice one. I just have a hunch.

"But let's talk about this when you're sober," he says, interrupting my fantasies of little Liam. Or Big Liam. Please, Goddess, let it be Big Liam. He says, "Consent when drunk isn't consent, right?"

And then it dawns on me how badly this night has gone. I'm drunk. Drunk! I'm a terrible mother! How could I drink four red-headed sluts? How could I allow myself to get intoxicated when I have babies waiting at home? Well, toddlers and a hot babysitter, but still. Details.

A mother shouldn't get drunk, even if my date with Earl gave me plenty of incentive. I shouldn't drink until the girls are in college. Maybe not even until they're in grad school because what if they need a ride somewhere?

"Wait," I say. I step back from the warmth of Liam's body, and it makes me sad. "You had a crush on me?" And then before he can answer... "I swear to God this is the first time I've gotten drunk with the girls and I'm really sorry and embarrassed and so irresponsible, but I really appreciate all your help tonight."

He blinks a couple of times. He's a really sexy blinker, so I reach my hands up to just touch his eyelids.

"Ow!" he says.

I guess that touch was more like a poke.

"Wow," he says and I'm wondering if he's going to take back

that thing he said about crushing on me, even though that was one of the nicest things I've ever heard. "Why don't you sit on the couch, right here, with this blanket..." He sets me down and quickly wraps my seaside blue afghan around me. "And I'll make us a couple of coffees. A couple of really stiff coffees."

Then Liam disappears.

And I take a quick little nap.

————

Liam

Ten minutes later, I return to the living room with steaming coffee mugs in hand. I'm pretty sure she takes soy milk in her coffee, but I want to ask and not just assume. "Sadie?" I say when she doesn't move. And then I see it. She is passed out. Cold. She's breathing out of her mouth and there's this weird sound happening. Maybe it's a groan, or, wait. It's that deep laugh sound she made earlier. Holy fuck. She's fast asleep and she's laughing in her dream. It's fucking adorable.

I'm having a dilemma here. I've got this coffee and she's drunk. She needs to sober up. But she's fast asleep. Do I wake her? What's better? Sadie makes the decision for me when she bolts upright, screams "Salad!" and runs for the bathroom.

I set the coffees down and chase after her. It's not really a decision; it's just instinct. Blame it on spending half my waking moments with little kids who constantly amaze me with what the human body is capable of producing. So this plot twist doesn't faze me a bit. I follow her into the bathroom and gently take her hair in my hands and hold it up and away as she barfs.

There are some details here that I won't go into, but let's just say there are sounds. And pleading. And then she's thanking some goddesses or something.

I let go of her hair, wet a washcloth with warm water, and

hand it to her. "You okay?" I ask. She nods. I help her to her feet. She's a little more steady.

"Do you want to clean yourself up?" I ask. She nods again.

"Shower," she says. "Brush my teeth."

"You steady enough?"

She looks me in the eyes and nods again, her lip trembling a little. She is steady enough. "You want me to grab you something to...." I ask.

"Change into? Would you? If you go up to my room, I have some pajamas in the top drawer."

I nod and close the door behind me. Immediately the shower turns on.

I creep upstairs, check on her girls to make sure they're breathing. They are. And then head to the only other room up there. God. Sadie's bedroom. How many times have I dreamed of being in here? Plenty, let me tell you.

Look in her underwear drawer! fourteen-year-old Liam squawks. It's super tempting, but if I find out what kind of underwear she wears I want it to be because she's showing me and not because I'm a creeper.

Looking in her top drawer is enough to get me semi-hard. All these silky fabrics. It's like she dresses in scarves or something. I pull out a pair of silky shorts and a camisole and then realize Sadie didn't ask me to grab any underwear. I'm holding pajamas that Sadie, who is in the shower lathering her curvy-as-fuck body, is going to put on without anything underneath. And my semi turns into a full-fledged cannon, ready to fire.

I must not think of Sadie lathering herself, or that I'm holding pajamas that are going to be nestled up where I'd like my face to be.

This hard-on isn't going anywhere.

I'm doomed.

Sadie

"Sober," I say into the mirror. "So. Brrrrr." Am I there yet? Nope. But the coffee will help.

But, man, am I paying for those sluts.

That sounds offensive, so I let out a drunken snort. Can you offend yourself? Is that a thing?

There's a knock on the bathroom door, and Liam says, "I grabbed some pjs for you." I open the door and his arm reaches in holding some shorts and a camisole. I should've asked him to grab me some underwear but that just seemed, I don't know, a little too intimate. Guess I'll sleep without. I grab the pjs from him and his arm disappears. Sad. I was starting to like the company.

I'm feeling a little more like myself. Steady. Solid. Dependable. Boring. I put on my pajamas and twist my hair up into a towel. Whatever makeup I had on has all washed away, along with the bad taste from my evening with Earl. *Earl*. What was I even thinking? Maybe I'm just not ready to date. Maybe that part of my life is done with.

That's depressing, though.

Liam is sitting on the couch, flipping through *Psychology Today*, surrounded by pillows. He looks good on my couch. Like he belongs there.

I shake that idea off.

"Thank you so much," I say. "For, uhm, everything."

"No sweat." He stands up. He's awkward all of a sudden and suddenly I see young Liam there, the Liam of that summer I watched him and all his siblings.

"I'm sure your crush on me is fully cured after witnessing that little episode." I motion to the bathroom. "I'm so embarrassed."

"There's no need to be. I've had plenty of those nights, especially when I was an undergrad. Maybe you needed to let loose a little."

I consider this. He's right. I've spent way too much of the last year being perfect and dependable, and that's not sustainable or healthy. One must strive for balance. Or at least that's what my fortune cookie said yesterday. "Maybe I did need to let loose. Sorta. As practice?" I say.

"Okay then. I think I'll just..."

"Head out?"

"Yeah," he says.

"Yeah," I say.

"I made you coffee, but it's cold."

"That's okay. That's sweet. I'll heat it up. I think I'll make something to eat before heading to bed. Soak up the residual alcohol."

There's a little pause here and we listen to the baby monitor. The tick of the house.

Liam grabs his bag and heads for the door.

"See you later," he says. Just before heading out he says, "Hey. How do you take your coffee?"

"With soy milk. No sugar," I say.

He nods and smiles and then disappears into the night.

I heat up the coffee. Make some toast with natural peanut butter.

I sit on the couch, in the same place Liam occupied a few minutes ago, and think I can still catch the scent of him. You'd expect something musky or piney, but Liam, as always, is a surprise. He smells like lemons. I love lemons.

Before I head to bed, I realize he never agreed with me about the barfing curing him of his childhood crush.

Even if I've scared him off, it helps me to know I was the star in someone's fantasy once, even if only for a while.

6 ULTERIOR MOTIVES

Liam

OVER THE WEEKEND I run seven miles, read four academic articles, and then visit my parents. Since my parents are a couple of nightmares, afterwards I run another eight miles just to clear my head.

On Sunday I go to the climbing gym, and work out until every muscle in my body is shaking. But even so, if anyone asked me, "Hey, Liam! What did you do this weekend?" the only honest answer would be that I thought about Sadie.

Seriously. I'm Mr. One Track Mind when it comes to her.

I thought about kissing Sadie for fifteen miles of running. And I thought about stripping her naked while I collated three hundred mailers for my father's political campaign. And on that climbing wall? I thought about fucking her in the shower. And on the bed. And on a picnic blanket.

Even while reading scientific research she was whispering in the back of my head. *Fuck me, Liam.* Someday she'll say that for real. It's going to happen.

The weekend went fast, seeing that every waking hour and

some of the sleeping ones were dedicated to ravishing her. And it wasn't fourteen-year-old Liam making the plans. Twenty-nine-year-old Liam has learned a few things about how to please a woman. If she gives me the chance, I'm going to pleasure every square inch of her body. By the time I'm done, she'll be moaning my name and begging me to marry her.

Whoa, okay. Not sure where that last idea came from. Let's walk before we run. But I'm very invested in her. Always have been. If I kept a To-Do list, Sadie would be at the top of it. And she would have stayed there for the last fifteen years.

It isn't until Monday that I'm able to put her out of my mind. A guy can't chase toddlers and think about sex at the same time. And that's a good thing. My poor libido needs a break, and these kids deserve my full attention.

Sadie's daughter Amy is clingy today. Maybe she's coming down with a cold. Usually she lives by the Ernest and Julio Gallo saying: we will have no whine before its time. But today she's whining it up with the best of them. At nap time, she won't lie in her crib with Piggypoo. I have to rock her in the chair until she passes out on my shoulder.

I close my eyes and relax under the warm weight of her little body. I let the rocking chair slow to a stop and just breathe. There are few moments of perfect stillness in a daycare setting. But the quiet in the room is a testament to the trust these little kids show us. They close their eyes because they know we're here to watch over them.

My little brother is at the top of an office tower somewhere making buckets of money trading derivatives. Whatever those are. My father is a rich lawyer who's running for a judgeship. That's the kind of job they expected me to get, too. "We raised you to be a leader, son," my father often says.

He doesn't understand, though, that my interest in childhood development is a direct response to the way he raised me. Or, rather, to the way he didn't. Nannies raised me. And babysitters.

My parents were a power couple—two corporate lawyers out to conquer the world. I swear they only had children so we could look good on their Christmas cards.

I grew up with nannies, and those women were amazing. Wanda, who was with us from the time I was two until I was twelve, still calls me every year on my birthday. She taught me to read and how to cook and how to take care of the people I love.

My mother taught me... God. How to yell at the interior designer. How to order wine. How to look the other way when your husband strays.

Most kids, though, don't have their own Wanda. There are millions of American kids in daycare. They matter, too. So I'm doing some graduate work in child development, with daycare as a focus. This job at Small Packages is part of my research. As someone who spent a lot of time being watched over by paid help, I'm trying to give back.

Also, little kids are hilarious. Who wouldn't want to make macaroni art professionally?

Amy shoves a thumb in her mouth and sighs. I listen to her soft breathing and feel at peace.

———

A day later, I'm watching the daycare door for Sadie. Like always.

But last night she ducked me. Somehow she arrived while I was busy with Blade and his dad. So Sadie did checkout with Mary Jane—the other sitter in the two-year old room. And she did it fast, too. By the time I said goodbye to Blade, she and the twins were gone.

It's not easy to gather up two squirmy toddlers, an assortment of lunch gear, extra clothing, and one stuffed pink pig in ninety seconds, flat, either. That's like ninja-level toddler management.

So I know she's avoiding me.

Tonight, though, she's going to have to speak to me. I have a permission slip that I need her to sign for her girls.

Naturally there are other things we'll need to discuss. I'm going to be the guy who breaks her dry spell. Maybe she thinks I was just kidding, or maybe she doesn't even remember the conversation. But I'm not going to let her duck me forever.

I walk around the room, tidying up. I break up a wrestling match between Kate and Amy. Both their faces are red and crabby. "What's the problem, girls? Is there a toy that needs sharing?"

They look at me and then back at each other. It's that hour of the day when you can wrestle your sister to the ground and not remember why.

"I need help with the copy machine," I tell them. "Somebody needs to push the big green button for me."

"My do it!" Kate yelps.

"No," Amy says.

"I could use both your help," I explain, because I am not a stupid man. "Amy, get Piggypoo and meet me by the door. Kate, come here now."

I scoop up Kate, step over the half-door and carry her to the copy machine. My permission slip is already on the uptake tray. "Bombs away, sister."

She pushes the big green button and the machine hums to life.

"Awesome. Now it's your sister's turn."

I swap kids and repeat this little procedure. That's when Sadie comes through the door. Because I'm standing in a different spot than usual, I have a perfect view as she tiptoes toward the two-year-old room and peeks around the doorframe.

"Looking for us?" I say, sneaking up on her.

Sadie jumps. "Hi, Liam! I didn't expect to see you over there; usually you're in the middle of the two-year-old room in the middle of the two-year-olds," she stays much too quickly.

"Why Sadie, I believe you're avoiding me." I smile, because

she's just so freaking cute. Even before I finish the sentence, her cheeks are on fire.

"Why would that be? It's not like I got rip-roaring drunk and puked all over the place while you held my hair." She lets out a little groan. "Over the weekend I actually considered shopping for another daycare center. Just so I wouldn't have to look you in the eye."

Oh, please. If I have my way, it won't be just my eyes she's looking at. But we'll get to that later. "You wouldn't deprive me of Kate and Amy's company just because of a little puke, would you?"

"If it didn't make me a horrible mother, I probably would." Her smile is sheepish. "And it wasn't just a little puke. It was..." She gulps. "Nevermind." She declines to finish that thought, and yet her eyes take a quick trip to my chest, as if she remembers fondling my muscles.

I grin.

She looks away.

"Look, Sadie. Eyes up here. I have a couple of things to catch you up on. Childcare things."

Reluctantly she turns my way again. Amy is reaching for her mother, so I hand her over. Then I unlock the half-door so we can all go inside and grab the girls' things.

"First of all, Amy was little happier today."

"She wasn't happy yesterday?"

"Not so much, no. Which I would've told you if you hadn't run out of here like the place was on fire."

"Oh," Sadie sighs. "She *was* a little sad last night. But I don't think she's sick." Sadie sets her daughter down and waits for the little girl to wander off before she finishes the thought. "My ex-husband was supposed to spend all of Sunday with the girls."

"And he didn't?"

"Yes and no. He told them he was taking them to the zoo. But then he realized that required a bit of actual effort, so he took them to the playground near our house instead. He spent 45 minutes of his precious time with his two children, before dropping them off again. When I saw his car pull up in front of my house, I assumed he'd forgotten something. But no. He'd had his fill of parental responsibility."

Ugh. That asshole. I hope I never meet him. "Amy was upset?"

"She was. They're too little to articulate it, but they know when a promise has been broken."

Having been on the wrong end of many such promises, I totally get it. "I'm so sorry about that. But she seemed okay today."

"Good. I'm done announcing his visits, though. Half the time when I tell them Daddy's coming, he lets them down." She crosses her arms over her luscious chest. "What else?"

Have sex with me. Lots of it. But that's a conversation we'll have another time. "Here." I show her the forms I've copied. "These are for you to read, and hopefully to sign."

"What is it? A permission slip?"

"For participating in my study."

"Your...?" She looks baffled.

"I'm doing research. For my Ph.D. in childhood development."

Now her eyes bug out. "You're in graduate school?"

"Sure. I'm working here for a year while I do research. And I've helped to design a global study which attempts to analyze how easily children can learn a task when it's taught to them by a human, versus by a video."

"Wow," she whispers. "What a cool thing to study!"

"Yeah. We want to learn whether videos are useful teaching tools or whether we're sacrificing our toddlers' attention spans for the sake of convenience."

"Yes! And what about eye contact?" she asks. "And normalized reactive traits!"

"Oh, baby," I whisper. "Whisper it in my ear."

Sadie laughs, low and throaty, and I feel it in my cock. "I had no idea you were a nerdy academic."

"The nerdiest. This fall I'm going overseas to work on the big group project. Sixty Ph.D. candidates in fifteen locations, testing kids on two continents."

Her eyes widen. "Wow. Where are you headed?"

"I don't know yet. We got to list our top choices, but the letters don't go out for a few weeks. The UK maybe. Or Rome." I nudge her with my elbow. "You thought I was just an hourly child-care worker, huh? No ambition?"

She tilts her head to the side and smiles. "I thought that was really nice, actually. There should be more Liams in childcare."

I think so, too. And now we're just standing here smiling at each other like fools.

That's when Kate does a face plant off the playhouse, landing with a thud that is going to haunt my dreams.

"Oh my God!" Sadie gasps as we both dash over there. Sadie gets there first, scooping her daughter off the rug before the first scream.

And it's a doozy.

"Oh, baby. Oh, sweetheart. I'm so sorry," she croons.

It's all my fault. I'm such an asshole for not paying attention before these kids are out of my care.

I swoop over and get Kate to show me her owey. She's crying and she's got a little rug burn on her forehead. "Kate," I say in my serious voice.

She stops crying for a beat and looks at me. Tears just on the edge of spilling over.

"I think this requires a Golden Band-Aid!" Then I do jazz hands. Actual jazz hands.

Kate's frown turns into a smile and those tears magically dissipate. Amy gasps a little at the significance of this moment. A Golden Band-Aid is highly coveted in this childish kingdom. It's a sign that you have an injury and you are *tough*.

I head over to the first aid kit and return with the Golden Band-Aid on a plush velvet pillow. It's just a regular Band-Aid with a gold sticker on it, but the kids imbibe it with magical power. I place it gingerly on her forehead. It doesn't really cover the rug burn, but that's not the point. "All better?" I ask.

"I'm tough!" she says.

"Golden Band-Aid tough!" And we fist bump with a nice boom at the end of it.

Sadie looks at me. "Thanks," she says softly.

I offer to help her load the girls and all the gear into her car, but Sadie politely declines. She's gone from view in a few minutes.

And I never got her to sign the paperwork I need for my study.

I smile. *Perfect.*

7 ACHIEVEMENT UNLOCKED

Sadie

"NO, you shouldn't keep dating him. Not with all those red flags!"

I'm on the phone with my baby sister, Megan, and she's asking me for advice. This is part of our routine. Weekly check-ins that help us stay connected but fall just short of being enough. I miss her, even when she's making terrible choices.

"But he's so cute," she whines. "He's a doc-torrrr."

"Yet he's emotionally un-avaaaaaaailable," I sing back.

"I don't want to marry him, Sadie. I just want to fuck him a little longer."

"Megan!"

She sighs.

It's a shame that we have to have this conversation over the phone. I'm angling for her to move back to Grand Rapids, but she insists that Atlanta is the place to be right now for actors. There's a zombie TV show she's trying to get cast in.

"Please don't let this man break your heart," I repeat, strongly and firmly in my mom voice, since my therapist voice has no effect on her. "When a guy runs so hot and cold, it's a sign. If he loves you on Monday and then doesn't return your texts on Tuesday, he's probably a raging narcissist. A nice guy doesn't string women along like that..."

"He's got a big dick..." she adds.

"Meg!"

She takes a deep inhale that makes me wonder if she's smoking. What, I'm not exactly sure. She's a bit of a wild child. And she does not have a good track record with dating. It's like she's choosing guys from the *Hi! I'm An Asshole* catalog. "You're right," she says eventually. "This is probably going to end badly."

"Gosh, you think?"

"But Sadie! I'm really..." She's searching for the word, I can tell. Lonely? Unsatisfied with her gypsy lifestyle? "Horny," she concludes. Aren't we all, I wonder. "Plus," she continues, "he's super hot. Like, *Grey's Anatomy* hot."

I can understand her dilemma.

"You say you just want a sexual relationship, but every time you try it, it turns out badly," I say. "I mean you can, of course, it's your life, but maybe try something different? Maybe try actually dating for a while...with *no* sex, and see if the guy is actually worthy of you."

"Worthy of me," she says and giggles.

"Worthy of you!" I repeat. "You are amazing and you deserve someone who will stop looking in his own mirror and worship you." I could use a little of that myself, I think. "Why don't you date that other guy you mentioned?"

"What guy?" she asks.

I'm having trouble remembering his name. She's been interested in a lot of guys over the years. "That guy you met at Jimmy John's?"

She laughs. "It's not a guy *at* Jimmy John's. It's a guy *named* Jimmy John. And no. Ew. He's not my type. He's, like, twenty-two and plays baseball."

"And that would be a problem because..." I really don't understand Meg sometimes.

"Because," she says all exasperated like. "I like my men older, wiser, and more experienced."

There's something in there that gives me pause. "You really like *older* men?" I ask tentatively, just testing it out. "They don't scare you with their...potential..." What am I afraid of here? "Oldness?"

She laughs again. "I love you to pieces, sis. But no. Older guys are just more interesting. And they know how to go down on a girl and do more than windshield wiper their tongue. God, I fucking hate windshield wipers."

I don't comment on that because I wouldn't know. Decker was not adventurous down south. He was mainly northern. And when he did take a rare trip south of the Mason-Dixon Line, it felt almost like he was using his tongue to press an elevator button that wasn't showing up.

"Sorry to change the subject on who you should *be intimate with*," I whisper. I don't want the girls to hear this conversation. "But it should not be that doctor."

"Okay," she says, but I'm not sure she means, *Okay, I agree with you*, or *Okay, let's move on*.

So I just move on.

"Do you think there are men out there who...like...older...women?" I venture.

Megan immediately reacts and jumps to conclusions. They're the right conclusions, but still. "Whoa there, sis! Who's made a pass at you? And why are you on the phone with me and not fucking him into tomorrow?"

Well, damn. She knows me too well. I thought I could just slide that question through, and she'd give me a hypothetical answer. And I can't ask Ash and Brynn without them guessing that I'm thinking about Liam. The hunky hunky Liam.

"Um, speaking of tomorrow, what are your plans?"

"DON'T CHANGE THE SUBJECT. WHO IS THE YOUNG STUD?"

"Shush!" I say into the phone. "Or the girls will come running."

Right now they're entertained with thinking putty and some Mozart on the stereo. Kate, by the way, has already forgotten her epic face plant. She stopped complaining the moment I handed her a little container of yogurt raisins and goldfish crackers. She happily ate the crackers and then spat the raisins across the room, one by one.

Both girls thought that was *hysterical*. And I let her get away with it because of her near miss with a head injury.

"Who. Is. He?" my sister hisses.

"It's..." Oh man. Do I tell her? "Do you remember Liam McAll..." I don't even give her the last name before she's freaking out. I literally have to hold the phone away from my ear while she's shrieking things like HOLY FUCK. And HE'S SO FUCKING DOPE and then there's some more swearing.

"Ow," I complain when she quiets down. "Is that kind of volume necessary?"

"Yes! Because Liam made a pass at my big sister. He grew up so fucking fine." She sighs.

"Don't I know it."

"Tell me everything. Where did you see him? Was there flirting? Or did he actually just come out and offer to put some motion in your ocean?"

"My..." That is not an appealing metaphor. "He babysat the girls one night when I went out on a date who turned out to be a loser. And, well, I told him it had been...a while. And he offered to help me out with my dry spell."

"I'm hyperfuckingventilating," she says. "Saddle up, cowgirl. Do. It. And yes—it's a legit thing that some men love cougars. And that's what you are, right? The horny divorcee out for the prowl for the young stud, ready to educate him and..."

"Although," I say, and really quietly I add, "I threw up in front of him, so he probably doesn't want to sleep with me anymore. And all of this is just hypothetical anyway," I offer, even though it clearly isn't.

"You threw up?" she asks, sounding concerned. "Flu?"

"No, sluts," I say. "Hold on a sec." I hear a knock at the door and peer around the corner. I only have to see his outline standing in front of the screen door to know. It's Liam. I can smell lemons in the air and if I had a penis, it'd be waving hello. "Remember, no messing around with marrieds! Gotta go!" I say and hang up on her. She'll forgive me. Because we're sisters.

I hear the scampering of the girls' feet and then a chorus of *Liams*. "Come in!" I call, but the girls have already swung the door open and have grabbed ahold of him like piranha starting to feed. God, are they actually biting him? That would be terrible.

I wonder if I could join in?

"Hi!" I say then add, "again."

The girls have grabbed hold of his forearm and now he's lifting them and lowering them repeatedly. Holy shit. Hello, muscles! "Hope I'm not interrupting," he says.

"Nope. Not at all." *I was just talking to my sister about how badly I want to jump you. No biggie.* There's no way he could have heard me from the front porch, right? My cheeks heat even though I know it's impossible. "The girls and I were just about to take a walk," I invent. But they could use a walk. It's warm out and we're only a couple of blocks from the park.

"Mind if I join you?" He grins and so obviously I can't refuse. Having already done ten arm lifts with the girls, he lowers them to the floor. "Oh, but before we head out, any chance you can sign that paperwork for me? If you're comfortable with the study. No pressure."

Oh. For some reason I'd thought this was a social call. I'm weirdly disappointed that he had another reason to see me. "Of course. No problem. I would've signed it at the center but..."

"Face plant," he says.

"Golden Band-Aid!" Kate screams.

"I want Gold Band-Aid," Amy says.

He squats down and looks her in the eyes, very seriously. "One day, I promise you, Amy, it will happen."

"When?" she asks.

"When you least expect it."

This seems to appease her. "Piggypoo," she says.

"Piggypoo can have one too, when that day comes."

She nods. They've come to an agreement. And I think my ovaries just pinged. Decker was never as tender, and never took the girls as seriously. *Stop it, ovaries.* No pinging allowed.

I sign the paperwork happily and hand it back to him. "So..."

"Walk?" he asks and I nod.

———

Liam

We're pushing the double stroller and the girls run on ahead of us, hair bouncing, Piggypoo flopping in Amy's arms. Kate's got her helmet on just in case she feels like tackling something. And she always feels like tackling something, usually me.

It occurs to me that a passerby would think we were a family out for an after-dinner summer stroll. The thought does not make my gonads retreat like it did in my early twenties. I've always wanted a family. I should be so lucky to have one with a woman like Sadie.

We're quiet for a bit listening to birdsong and the girls' feet running ahead of us.

"I have a confession to make," Sadie says. Fourteen-year-old Liam immediately reacts. *Please say you want to touch my boner! Pleeeeeease!*

I tell him to shut up. First, not appropriate. Second, there is no boner. Yet.

"And that is?" I ask all smooth like, because she can't hear my inner fourteen-year-old.

"My goal here is to utterly exhaust the girls so that when we're walking back, they're passed out happily in their stroller and will sleep soundly till dawn."

Is she going to take me up on my offer of curing her of her sexual drought? Because I am totally down with that. "Big plans tonight?" I ask lightly.

"My girlfriends are coming over. It's Netflix and cheesecake night."

"Netflix and cheesecake?"

"Yep. Ash brings the booze. I supply the movies. And Brynn brings a bunch of cheesecake. It's all she wants to eat right now."

"She's the pregnant one, right?"

"Yep. Any day now, we think, she'll pop."

"Sounds...painful."

Sadie rubs her hand across her forehead. It's hot and she's been pushing the stroller. I make a motion to her and she nods, letting me take over. "Let me guess," I say. "The cheesecake is gluten-free and vegan friendly?" I've noticed all the super healthy snacks she packs for the girls. Even gluten-free goldfish crackers.

"Hardly. Brynn cooks or bakes whatever she wants and we eat it. No questions asked."

"Sounds a little..."

"Fattening? You haven't tried her food. Once you do you'll understand. I mean, I'd say I'm about 75% vegetarian and organic and 25% Brynn. She's her own food group."

This is yet another reason why I really want to spend more time with Sadie, so I can get to know her friends. I want to know everything about her.

"Kate! Do not head-butt that tree!" Sadie calls.

Kate stops running and glares at Sadie.

"Why?!"

"What did that tree do to you?"

Kate thinks about it and then hugs the tree instead, then rushes to catch up to her sister. The park is just at the top of this hill. I can hear a baseball game in progress. Dogs barking. The creak of swings soaring toward the blue sky.

"I love this neighborhood," I sigh. "Kids need physical activity. People are so obsessed with early childhood learning, but kids at this age learn by moving their bodies. They can memorize the alphabet later."

"Exactly!" Sadie says, beaming. "And an early bedtime is good for me when I need some quiet time with my friends."

"Agreed. A happy mom is a better mom." And oh, how I could make her happy.

"Almost there!" Sadie pants as we climb the last few meters. "I thought we'd never make it. It's so hot!" I can see the shimmer of sweat on Sadie's warm, toned skin. It's probably beading in between her breasts, down her navel, between her legs...

Shut up, teen Liam!

As much as I want to envision Sadie's breasts, and her navel, and all the places I'd like to visit, I can't right now. I'm busy pushing this double stroller up a really big hill and flex my arm muscles at the same time. This is part of the mating dance. I'm off-gassing manly pheromones right now. It's science.

Finally we reach the shady playground, and the twins take off toward the sandbox first.

"Oh, hell." Sadie sighs. "Not the sandbox."

"Germs?" I guess.

"Germs aren't the problem," she says. "Dirt is natural. I do have a problem with all the sand they get in their shoes and socks. No matter how many times I vacuum, there's always more. It's like living at the beach, without the ocean view."

"I don't know how you do it all. The kids. The job. The house. Do you ever sleep?"

"Every other Tuesday," she says. "Kate! Don't put that sand down your pants!" She takes off running, and fourteen-year-old Liam admires her ass as she goes.

Twenty-nine-year-old Liam does, too.

———

An hour later we're walking back down the hill toward home. "Will you catch one, and I'll catch the other?" Sadie asks me when it was time to go, but the twins aren't willing to get into the stroller.

"Of course. Catching toddlers is literally my job."

"Yeah, but you're off the clock. You can snag Amy. She's easy."

"I'll tackle Kate," I offer. "I like a challenge."

Her pretty face gets a starry expression when I say this, which means my mating ritual is totally working. My lizard brain is calling out to her lizard brain. I read about that in *Nature*, once.

"Ready?" I say. "Go!"

Sixty seconds later we have two exhausted toddlers strapped into the stroller. Kate screams at the injustice, her little round face going red.

"No yellin'," her sister grunts.

About seven seconds later, they're both passed out, their two heads leaning toward one another, like a couple of bookends.

Sadie wipes her forehead with the back of her hand. "Thank you. That's so much easier with two people."

I'm sure it would be. So where the hell is her husband? What kind of guy can walk away from his wife and his own children? It boggles the mind. And the balls. If I were Sadie's man, she'd be pregnant with another set of twins, because I couldn't keep my hands off her.

Triplets, maybe.

"Can we stop a sec?" Sadie asks, pointing at an ice cream truck. "I need a bottle of water."

"Of course." I pull out my wallet. "Just water?"

"I'm saving myself for cheesecake."

"Ah, right." I buy a lemon ice for myself, which I drop into the stroller's cupholder, and also her bottle of water.

"Here." She holds out two singles to pay for it.

"Keep it," I say. Call me a caveman, but I'm unable to let Sadie pay.

"You've helped me enough," she insists, as I maneuver the stroller into the shade, where we can pause beside a tree at the edge of the park. I feel a small hand slide something into my back pocket.

I reach back, lightning fast, and catch her hand. "Are you trying to get in my pants?" I chuckle as I say it. But I swear a jolt of electricity moves through my body when I catch her hand in mine. And when I meet her gaze, I can tell she feels it, too.

"Liam!" she whispers, scandalized.

"Sadie!" I return, my fingers closing around her smoother ones.

The moment stretches and takes hold. The evening sunlight gives her skin a honeyed tone, and her eyes are bright and wide. Her lips part in surprise as I stroke her palm with my thumb. But she doesn't pull away.

We're like those cartoon characters with hearts in their eyes, both of us caught, just staring at each other. I can't stop admiring her rosebud mouth—the same one I used to fantasize about when I was a teenager. And there's a flush creeping up her cheeks. Like she can't help it, and she can't look away.

So I do the obvious thing. I lean forward and take her mouth in a kiss.

I've had a lot of practice kissing women. It's not bragging to say that I don't have trouble finding willing participants. And thank fuck for muscle memory, because my brain basically shorts out the second Sadie makes a little whimper of surprise.

That sound goes straight to my cock. So I raise the stakes,

stepping closer, owning her mouth with mine. Tasting her turns me into a brush fire. With my free hand, I reach around and pull her body closer.

Her lips part, and I don't miss a beat. I deepen the kiss, tilting my head to perfect the connection.

Meanwhile, fourteen-year-old-Liam practically strokes out. *Achievement Unlocked!* he screams as I meld my tongue to Sadie's, tasting her until she whimpers and throws her arms around my neck.

I've been waiting for this moment for fifteen years. So I spin around and pin her against the trunk of a tree. Then I give her one last, urgent kiss. Okay, three more.

But then I stop.

No, really. I pull myself back from the heat of Sadie's perfect mouth, and I look down at her. She's panting and red-cheeked, and looking up at me, dazed and desperate. "This is happening," I tell her.

"Wh-what is?"

"You and me. Naked on a bed. Or a kitchen counter, or in the shower."

She says, "unngh."

"I'll let you pick the room of the house. Or the backyard. But this is happening. Soon. Maybe this weekend."

"Liam, we couldn't possibly. The girls…"

"Are terrific sleepers," I point out, casting a meaningful glance into the stroller, where they're dead to the world. "This isn't about them. They'll never know. This is about you and me getting some exercise."

"Exercise?" she whispers.

"Oh hell yes. We both need some very energetic sex. You've been a nun for two years. And I've been waiting half my life to get you naked. Our time is now."

She swallows. Hard. And she looks awfully flushed.

"Here." I take the bottle of water out of the cupholder and twist off the cap. "Drink this and cool down."

She takes several gulps. "It's not working."

"That's because you know I'm right. There's only one way that fire you're feeling goes out." Her eyes widen, and I think four-teen-year-old Liam is impressed at this bit of persuasion. "There isn't a single reason why we can't get together this weekend for a night of no-strings sex. I'll pull out all the stops. But it's just for fun, right? If you don't enjoy yourself, we don't have to do it again."

Sadie fans herself.

"Saturday, then? Unless you have plans?"

"No pl-plans," she stammers. "But..."

"See you Saturday," I say. "Drink that water, okay? You look flushed."

Then I grab the lemon ice out of the cupholder, wave at Sadie with the plastic spoon, and turn around. I walk away, knowing her eyes are stapled to my ass. A weaker man would turn and check. But I don't need to.

Fourteen-year-old Liam runs off to make popcorn and waits to see what happens next.

8 NETFLIX, CHEESECAKE & COUGARS

Sadie

I CAN'T BREATHE. I really can't. And breathing is good, necessary even, especially when lugging two boneless toddlers and tucking them in for nighty night.

As I pull the stroller up to my back porch, I have one of those panicked moments when I have to choose who to bring inside first, and who waits in the backyard? Single-parenting twins is just plain hard. And even though I live in a safe neighborhood, it's not a choice I can make. So I prop the door open and start unbuckling the girls. I'll carry them at the same time, drawing on my inner feminine power to buck up and just do it.

Luckily, I don't have to. Just as I prop the door open, there's Ash and Brynn staring out at me. They're right in my personal space, and for a second it scares the shit out of me. And it also forces me to start breathing again, so....win?

"Hi," Brynn says.

"Hiiiiiiiiiii," Ash says, drawing it out.

I squint my eyes. Something is not right here. Not that they're already in my house—they know where the spare key is—but it's the way they're just standing there and smiling. Ash is nodding with this smirk on her face. Brynn is rubbing her belly like she's trying to make a genie come out. Who knows? Maybe she is. It is too hot to be pregnant right now.

"Hi?" I ask and then, "Ash, could you?"

She nods and walks to the stroller. I unstrap Amy and hand her to Ash who carries her like she's a bomb about to explode if she jostles it too much. Amy wouldn't explode; she'd just cry after being startled. Kate's the one you need to watch out for.

We quietly creep upstairs, tuck the girls in, and then I'm breathing normally again. I'm not even feeling Liam's hot, supple lips against my own. Nope. Not one bit. Or imagining a different kind of kiss from him. One that's a little lower? A lot lower? More intimate? Gosh. Can't I just say it? One on my clitoris.

"You're all red," Ash says, but she says it in this weird way, like she knows something.

"It's ninety degrees out and 99% humidity. And I just took the girls on a massive walk."

"Uh-huh."

I don't answer her. We just walk downstairs, careful not to make any noise. We need a Netflix and cheesecake night like nobody's business.

Or maybe that's just me.

Moments later we're settled onto the sofa while Brynn opens a couple of containers. She pops something into her mouth and moans. "This is so good. I've outdone myself, I think." She quickly swallows. "I brought an appetizer, the main course, and a dessert."

"Oh wow!" I say. "I wasn't expecting a full dinner!"

"Wellllll, technically it's not dinner. It's three different cheese-cakes. The goat cheese and onion tart is the appetizer. New York-style cheesecake is dinner. And the dessert is chocolate cheese-cake with strawberries and whipped cream."

Ash moans, too. "We're really living the dream here, ladies."

We all nod.

Once we've loaded up our plates and I've poured some kombucha—it's really good for the gut flora—we collapse in the living room, ready to veg out.

"What are you guys in the mood for?" I ask, bringing up the Netflix icon on my screen.

"Hmmm..." Ash says. "I dunno. How about something sexy? Like, *The Graduate!*"

That's a little weird. Usually Ash asks for some kind of action flick involving explosions or car chases or both.

"Nah," Brynn says. "I'm much more in the mood for *American Pie*. You know, I think that's the movie where the term MILF was invented. You know, a Mother I'd Like To Fuck."

There's a massive scoop of New York-style cheesecake hovering just inches from my mouth when everything clicks into place. "Dammit!" The fork clatters to my plate. "What did you guys see?"

They both collapse in hysterics. Seriously, they're laughing so hard that Brynn might go into labor. I should've known when I entered the door and they were al *oh, hiiiiiiii*. And Brynn's eyebrows were wagging. And Ash was all smirky. They must've seen Liam kissing me! They must've driven right past and I was so involved I didn't even notice.

"Just tell us if that runner boy is as good a kisser as I imagine him being."

And I get a little bit jealous all of a sudden when Ash says that. Like my inner goddess growls *mine*.

"Please say there's more where that kiss came from!" Brynn this time. "Please tell me there is boinking. I can't boink right now. It's just too much effort, but I'd love to live vicariously through you."

"No! There's no...boinking." I clear my throat, set the cheesecake down. "Or blowing. Or banging. Or anything. It was just a kiss."

Ash shakes her head. "I know what a just-a-kiss looks like, and that was not. That's was just-a-foreplay. That dude wants you so bad."

"Liam," I say, and I sort of sound all breathy and ridiculous.

"*Liammm*," they echo, mimicking me in the same voice.

Fucking girlfriends.

"So..." I should probably just tell them. They're my best friends and they've always been my support system. They'll tell me the truth and be real with me, and consider all the options. They won't jump to conclusions and I know I can trust them.

So why am I procrastinating? Why don't I just blurt it out?

"Liam wants to have a no-strings-attached sexual relationship with me to cure me of my sex drought and because apparently it will fulfill some inner fantasy he's had of me since he was fourteen."

This is the part where my besties ponder the question with me. We'll have an in-depth conversation discussing the pros and cons and the possible emotional complications, and...

Ash says, "Do it."

Brynn says, "Yeah. Fuck him."

Ah. That was fast. "But aren't I too..."

"Short?" Brynn guesses. "Nah."

"Uptight?" Ash supplies. "Didn't look like it a half hour ago."

"...*Old*," I finish. "He makes me feel like a cougar."

"You can't be a cougar until at least forty," Ash says. "It's a rule. So you have five years left. But in five years he'll be thirty-four, and the differential between your ages will be inside of twenty percent. So you will have aged out of cougardom."

"You'll be fully amortized," Brynn adds.

We both give her weird looks. "Do you know what amortized means?" Ash asks.

"No, but it sounds like the Latin word for love." She shrugs. "Let's eat cheesecake and watch a kissing movie."

And that is why the three of us have never successfully completed a serious conversation. We have, on the other hand, successfully completed many a cheesecake.

9 NOOKIE

Sadie

THE REST of the week goes by way too slowly. Liam manages to be assisting other parents every time I turn up at daycare. But even if we don't speak, I practically burst into flames every time we're in the same zip code.

Maybe it's just my thighs rubbing together, causing extra friction.

Nope. It's the sight of Liam. That messy hair. Those shoulders. That firm chest. Those blue eyes.

Gah!

I honestly can't picture myself leading him to my bedroom for a casual night of sex. I mean, how do I even do that? "Come here big fella? Come to momma?"

Too much eww.

Maybe the ability to seduce a man in bed just shrivels up after you've been off the market a few years. Like, I don't know, how in science fiction movies someone gets their life essence sucked out of them and they're left a desiccated sheath. Maybe that's what I am. A desiccated sheath.

Maybe all of this is moot anyway. Maybe he didn't mean any of it. Maybe...

Friday evening he texts me just after I've put the girls to bed. And the minute my phone lights up with his name, I feel a shimmy of excitement. Tomorrow is Saturday, and maybe he was serious? He means to water my sexual dry spell?

He texts: *Should I bring over dinner tomorrow? I'll bet the girls would love my butter chicken*.

Hmmm.

I can't have the girls getting used to having Liam around. Also, they'd never settle down if he was there. And how can I do a no-strings thing if he's cooking for me?

This would have to be an after-bedtime kind of thing, I tap back. *You're too distracting*.

You're pretty distracting yourself, he writes back. *I've been on the same chapter of this book all week. Can't seem to read, because I'm thinking about undressing you tomorrow night*.

Just reading those words gives me a crazy thrill. I can't decide if I'm more excited or more terrified. It could really go either way. Dammit, though. I'm really doing this.

I text: *I'll leave you a beer on the porch, and you can wait there until the coast is clear. The house will be quiet by 7:15 or 7:30*. I can't believe I'm actually working out the logistics, as if this is really happening.

I'll be waiting, he says.

Three words, and I feel hot all over.

Saturday only gets worse. It's a hot, sticky day, which turns into a sultry evening. At seven o'clock I put two beers in an ice bucket and leave them on my front porch.

At one minute past seven I have a nervous breakdown.

Maybe that's a slight exaggeration. But I feel jittery and wired as I supervise bath time, wrestle the girls into their summer pjs, and then read three picture books. The AC is on full blast, but I feel warm anyway.

"Night night, sweetie," I whisper to Amy. "Night, Kate." I tuck the girls into bed, and they go down easily. It must be all that running around we did at the playground today. And the obstacle course. And the trampoline park. I wasn't taking any chances.

Still, I linger outside their door for a while, just to be sure.

But ten minutes later I'm sure they're asleep. So now I'm just stalling. I go into my bathroom and brush my teeth vigorously. As if that makes me more appealing. Younger. Less squishy in the midsection.

Gah. This is too much pressure. I haven't been naked with a man for the first time in... Wow. I'd need a calculator to count that high. A long time. As I run a brush through my hair, an involuntary shiver of fear snakes down my spine. What if Liam doesn't really know what he's in for? He might be picturing the twenty-year-old me. Once he sees the goods up close, he might recoil in horror.

I sneak a peek in the mirror. *Okay. Not bad*, is my first reaction. I still have rich, wavy hair and a face that I've been protecting with sunscreen for thirty-four years.

But. There's a splotch of spaghetti sauce on my top. So I shuck that off and toss it into the hamper. Then I'm confronted with the real trouble—a body that gave birth to twins. I no longer have the tiny waist of my youth. And there are scars on my belly. If I take off my bra, my boobs will show signs of gravitational pull.

So that's settled. This bra is staying on no matter what. Not getting my breasts naked. Nope. Nope. Nope. On second thought, maybe *all* my clothes will stay on.

Maybe Liam should go home. This is the worst idea I've ever had.

My breathing gets all shallow and shaky as I look for a clean top in my closet. I choose a sleeveless thing that's not trying too hard. I don't want to look nervous.

I'm fucking terrified.

The best thing to do is to go downstairs, drink a beer with

Liam on the porch, and then tell him very sweetly that I'm just not ready. He's a good guy. He'll respect that.

Yeah. That's the solution.

I trot down the stairs and open the front door. And there he is, sitting on a wicker chair, the neck of a beer bottle between two of his thick fingers. He looks hotter than an August afternoon in khaki shorts and a polo shirt that's straining to accommodate his biceps. He looks up at me and winks. "Hello, gorgeous."

Oh, my. I get a happy little shiver at the sound of his voice. He is the sexiest being I have ever seen. Which is why we can't possibly have sex. "Liam," I begin.

"Yes, gorgeous?" He stands up, bringing his muscular self even closer.

"We need to talk."

"I'll bet." He grabs the ice bucket and steps into my personal space. Then he nudges me back into the house with a smile. "You're going to give me a little speech about how you're not ready, right?" He shuts the door behind himself.

"Um, well..." I let out a nervous giggle. "Something like that."

"I see..." He walks past me and into my living room. He sets the ice bucket on the floor beside the coffee table and sits down on the couch. "Here's the deal. We're going to talk for five minutes. And if you still feel that way, I'll leave immediately."

"Five minutes," I repeat slowly.

"Sure. I'll set a timer. Come here, okay?" He pats the sofa beside him and then taps his smartwatch a couple of times.

I knew he'd understand. Liam is going to be a catch for some woman someday. I sit down beside him and let out a breath. I already feel a little calmer.

And then the room spins. Or, rather, Liam has scooped me off the couch, turned me around as if I weigh no more than Amy's Piggypoo, and deposited me onto his lap, where I'm now straddling him.

"So let's talk," he says from way too close. I'm staring right into his endless blue eyes, and his kissable mouth is mere inches away. "Tell me what's the problem?"

"Well..." I clear my throat. "The problem seems to be..."

Okay, I don't remember. Because Liam dips his head until his lips find the sensitive skin just in front of my ear. He nibbles it with his lips. There should be a word for that maneuver. He *nipples* it.

And now I'm thinking about nipples. Mine, mostly. My breasts are brushing against his tight body. Liam's mouth finds my neck. He slowly places a hot, open-mouthed kiss there.

I grab his big shoulders and gasp. Nobody has kissed my neck in a million years. It feels so good that I whimper.

Liam chuckles, and the sound brings me back to reality.

"We're supposed to be talking," I slur. But his lips... Gah. I'm turning into a liquid.

"So talk," he says in a husky voice. "I'm listening."

"I can't get naked with you."

"Okay, fine."

Okay, fine?

I'm trying to process this when Liam's mouth takes mine in a hungry kiss. It's a sneak attack, but his lips are so warm and firm that my eager body doesn't miss a beat. I'm kissing him back like it's my job. And I tilt my head to make sure we've got the best possible connection.

Then his tongue teases the seam of my lips. When I open for him, he tastes of cold beer and youth and the kind of fun I haven't had in a long time. Each kiss is a little deeper. And each one ends as another begins. Strong arms pull me closer to his body, and my brain clicks right off. Instead of thoughts, I hear static, like a dysfunctional baby monitor.

Kissing Liam is the best decision I never really made.

We go on and on until Liam makes a hungry sound deep in his chest. And that sound does some crazy things to my body. An electrical storm sizzles inside me, the current snapping between my breasts and my clenching legs. My hands begin to roam freely. They slide down the muscles of Liam's chest, my thumbs grazing the wide, flat nipples I feel beneath the cotton.

Then two things happen at the same time. Liam groans again, which makes my vagina contract. And his watch beeps.

Liam breaks our kiss and tilts his head back, resting it on the sofa. I just sit there on his lap, quivering, trying to catch my breath. "What were you saying?" he pants.

"No idea," I admit.

He smiles up at my ceiling. "I'll go home if you want me to. But I'd rather explore every inch of your body. With my tongue."

A shocked little noise escapes from my throat.

"If you want me to leave, you'll have to climb off my lap. But if you don't want me to leave, you can keep rubbing yourself all over me like that."

"I'm not..." I look down. "Oh hell I am."

"That would be even more fun without your shirt." Liam's hands wander up my back, under the cotton. "Couch or bedroom?"

"Um..." It's so *bright* in here. "Bedroom."

The second the word leaves my mouth, I'm airborne. Liam stands up suddenly, catching me with one arm under my bottom and one wrapped around my back. He pauses to kiss me. I wrap my legs around his waist and... Holy erection, Batman. Either Liam is really wound up or he's concealing a beer bottle in his shorts.

With his lips still tempting mine, he begins to thread his way around the sofa, heading toward the stairs. I have a brief moment of concern that he could trip on any number of toddler toys between the couch and my bedroom. But Liam has youth on his side, and he seems highly motivated. We arrive in my bedroom less than a minute later.

Liam deposits me on the bed and then whips off his shirt. "This is the best idea I've had in a *long* time," he says.

My mouth goes dry as I gaze up at the perfection that is Liam McAllister in all his shirtless glory. Then the view gets even better when he unzips his shorts and kicks them away. The only thing standing between me and Liam now is a very ambitious erection. It's poking out of the top of a pair of tight black boxer briefs.

"Holy mother of God," I whisper. There's a nearly naked sex god at the foot of my bed. And he's grinning at me like I've just said something funny.

"Your turn," he says.

I grip my cotton top in two hands and... That's when it all comes to a crashing halt. I can't do it. I can't whip off my clothes like he just did, and bare my belly to Adonis here.

"Sadie?" he asks gently.

"There's too many lights on," I blurt out. "Hang on a second." I leap off the bed, yank the curtains closed, and shut off the lights. I also lock the bedroom door. "That's so much better," I say, suddenly blind and stumbling toward the bed.

I stumble into Liam, fall against him. He catches me with an *oof* sound, and stumbles backwards a step or too. "Have a seat!" I squeak, sounding not at all hysterical.

"Okay," he says and I think I hear a smile in his voice.

What now? Almost-naked Liam is in my bed, waiting for me. It's pitch dark but I can *feel* his expectations, and they're all pointed at me.

But. Decker is suddenly in my head telling me how my post-partum body resembles a cow's. He literally said my lactating breasts turned him off.

I cannot let Liam see me naked, but I still really, really want to have sex with him. Like, bad.

"Sadie?" he asks.

I want to climb onto that bed. Hell, I want to climb onto Liam. But my limbic system, that old lizard brain responsible for flight or fight reactions and cortisol and all that good stuff, has kicked into high gear, and I'm just not able to work through it.

I'm only able to panic. But I do have one idea. "How do you feel about blindfolds?"

"Um, sounds like fun?" Liam says.

"I think so, too!" I say with false cheer. I sit down on the bed and reach out to touch him on the arm.

"Well, *hello*," he groans, sounding really fucking sexy.

Because I didn't grab his arm! His penis is in my hand. He took his shorts off and it's all penis. In my hand.

And, wow. Nice work, McAllister family genes. I pat him on the super-tight abs. "I thought, you know, we'd just experiment a little."

"With a blindfold?" he asks.

"Yup!" I climb onto the bed, though, because he feels so good, and I might need a few more of those kisses. For courage.

I straddle him and I...he's...Right. There. I'm still wearing clothes, but he is bare. And hard. And I rock just a little bit, feeling how good he is, how hard.

"Sadie," I hear a chuckle in his voice. He's *laughing* at me. I knew it. This was a terrible idea. He thinks I'm a joke. "Hot stuff, I know this is scary, but you've got to trust me here, okay. Do you trust me?"

I think about it and then I nod. I do trust him.

"Are you nodding or anything because I literally can't see anything."

"I'm nodding." So hard I think I might pass out.

"Then let's try this my way," he says.

I'm actually really relieved. My lizard brain is in complete freak-out mode, so it would be nice to calm that little beast down. "Okay," I say. "I'm all yours. Or at least I want to be. But I just, need to talk it out first. Is that okay?"

It's funny because as a therapist, I'm usually the one who listens, but right now, I need words.

"Talk?" he asks, but not in a disappointed tone. "Of course."

"Let me grab my robe. Just give me a second."

I stumble into the bathroom. In a burst of optimism, I take off my bra and panties and pull on a robe instead. If I locate my courage, at least I'll be ready. I do some deep yoga breathing to calm down. I splash some water on my face.

I am who I am. This is my body and I need to honor it. This is a body that has grown two children *at the same time* and if Liam isn't attracted to me, then he isn't. I don't need him to be attracted to me. I *want* him to be, but I don't need him.

All right then.

I take one more deep breath of courage, open the door, and there's Liam waiting for me. Only things have slightly changed.

10 THE LUCKIEST GUY IN THE WORLD

Liam

I CAN TELL Sadie is a little uncomfortable. I'm not sure if it's because of me, or it's something about herself, but I have a feeling her divorce is probably at the root of it somewhere. She's adorably awkward and unsure right now. I can't believe I'm finally in her bed, naked; fourteen-year-old Liam might pass out from excitement. But older, wiser Liam knows this is not a sprint. With Sadie, I actually want the marathon.

When she high-tails it to the bathroom, I put my boxers back on and then make a few changes to the room. I turn on a lamp to its lowest setting. I part the curtains enough to let in some dusky light. And then I open the windows. There's a lovely cross-breeze bringing in the scent of wildflowers and pine from the woods surrounding her home. A couple of taps on my phone and I've started some soft music playing.

When Sadie comes out of the bathroom, she has a floral robe on. The fabric is silky and falls over her skin like water. I honestly don't think she realizes how stunning she is, but man. She is. Like a goddess stepping from the shadow into moonlight.

She stands in the doorway of the bathroom, illuminated by the light behind her. Her shape is curvy and divine and I just want to wrap my arms around her. So I do. I just walk over to her, and surround her with my arms. She fits perfectly against me, like her body was somehow meant to curl up next to mine. We're a regular yin and yang.

I can actually feel her start to relax. "You want to talk? We don't have to do anything tonight, you know. This is a long-standing offer. No quick decisions." I'm about to tell her I'm in this for the long haul, but I catch myself just in time. If I say that out loud, I'll startle the both of us.

"I'm sorry," she says. "I'm feeling really vulnerable right now and it's scary."

I nod because I get it. "Come on." I lead her to the bed. I crawl in, and sit with my back against the headboard. She curls up next to me, snuggled in, her head on my chest. And as much as I want to make love to this woman, this other kind of closeness is pretty great, too.

"My ex...Decker," she starts, and I don't say anything. She needs me to listen. "He did a number on me. I thought we had the perfect life. Nice house, great relationship, healthy girls. And while I had a kind of rosy glow about how nice our world was, and while I was enjoying motherhood, he couldn't join in. For him all the fun was over."

I make a rude noise, and then clap my hand over my mouth. "Sorry." But neither fourteen-year-old Liam nor twenty-nine-year-old Liam likes where this story is going.

"Decker couldn't see me as a sexual being anymore, but just as a...breeder, for lack of a better word. I waited. I thought he was giving me space. But he wasn't. It was like the plot twist in one of those horror movies we loved to watch together. Decker was busy falling in lust with our nanny, and banging her on our living room sofa."

The upset noise tries to escape me again, but I tamp it down.

"It's *so* cliché and embarrassing. And I just think that maybe, if I had been more..." She pauses here and I feel her tense. I stroke the top of her head, my hand lacing through her soft hair. "If I had just been *more* he would've been happy."

We just sit with that for a second. I'm trying to process what she said. Finally, I ask, "Were you happy?"

"Yeah. I mean..." She bites her lip. "Parenting is hard, and I was willing to power through the rough patches. But he didn't want me anymore. And the result is that now I can't take off my clothes with *you*. Because I can still see the look of revulsion on his face when I suggested that eleven months was too long to go without sex."

Ouch. "So maybe you're *not* ready." I run a finger down her cute nose. "Maybe you don't need the stress of forcing yourself through it right now."

"Yeah," she says quietly, and part of me is disappointed. The erect part. "Yeah. Except... Then he wins."

"No." I shake my head vehemently. "I'm positive he already lost. The minute he walked away from you and your girls."

"Maybe." Her face says she doesn't believe me. "But he took my self-esteem with him."

"You'll find it again," I promise.

"Sure, someday. But in the meantime I won't get any more of those kisses from you."

Her pretty eyes lift to study me, and I can't help but smile. "That is a risk."

"Can I have one more? As a consolation prize? A party favor?"

"I'm right here." It takes all my willpower not to crush my mouth to hers again. But it has to be her choice. "Come and take it."

She props herself up on an elbow and studies me. "You're *so* beautiful. It's sort of shocking."

Back at you, babe. I'm dying right now as she runs her fingertip along my cheekbone.

"...Especially right here." She leans in and places a soft kiss at the corner of my eye. "And here." I get another kiss at the edge of my mouth. "And here, too..." She kisses my jaw.

I let out a groan, because I can't help it. "If I kissed you every-where *you're* beautiful, it would take all night. Maybe two."

Sadie's eyes widen with surprise. And then she kisses me for real. Soft lips fit against mine.

And I'm drowning. She kisses me again, sliding her body onto mine. I kiss her over and over again. I wrap my arms only lightly around her, because I don't want to overstep. But the silk of her gown is slippery over her curves, and my body is on fire. I've never been so turned on as our tongues stroke and meld together.

I don't think I will *ever* get enough. Because Sadie isn't just beautiful, she's passionate. She kisses me with the same intensity she had fifteen years ago when she used to tell me her thoughts. I saw that same fire in her every time she explained a movie scene or urged me to read one of her favorite books.

This is the same Sadie—pure joy and all focus. Our mouths are nothing but pleasure and heat. Our tongues dip and stroke in time with my heartbeat.

I've won some kind of karmic lottery. The woman of my dreams is kissing the hell out of me. Her hips have begun to undu-late against mine, like she can't get close enough.

I skim a palm down the silk of her gown until her breast is heavy in my hand. I stroke a thumb over her nipple and feel it pebble under my touch. "*Liam*," she pants into my mouth, and I wonder if I'm about to be reprimanded.

"Yeah?"

"I'm so *wet*."

"Are you sure?" I mumble against her lips. "Maybe I'd better check."

Smooth! my fourteen year-old-self cheers as I dip a hand between Sadie's legs.

But Jesus lord—men are wired to respond to a turned-on woman, and my body has a swift and powerful reaction. Because she's *drenched*. Like Hurricane Katrina level flooding. She moans as I coat my fingers in her desire, and slowly stroke her.

"So good. So good," she chants against my lips. Sadie eases her body on top of mine and kisses me. The weight of her is everything I've ever wanted. Then she rolls her hips. And I'm not prepared for the molten-hot bliss of Sadie Mathews doing a slow grind on my dick.

I need to come now. Sorry, says fourteen-year-old Liam.

"Oh no you fucking don't!"

"What?" Sadie asks, breathless.

Whoops. "I said, uh, maybe we need a condom. But it's totally your call." Meanwhile, I have to shove a hand into my boxer briefs and squeeze the base of my dick to keep myself in control. I bring up a mental image of my sixth-grade teacher's turkey-wattle neck skin while I try to calm down. It's been years since I needed that trick. But nobody thrills me like Sadie.

"Get the condom, Liam," she whispers. "Do it."

There are lasers that can't move as quickly as I do now. I kick off my briefs, grab the condom off the table where a left it earlier, flick off the wrapper, and roll it on. "Go," I wheeze.

YES! fourteen-year-old Liam screams. *Hide my salami!*

That's when I mentally drag him into a closet, toss him onto the floor, and then kick the door shut. *Later, buddy.* This is a job for a real man.

Sadie's trusting brown eyes bore into mine as she lines herself up above me. I cup her smooth cheek in one hand and smile at her as I tug her down for a kiss. Then she rocks my world by sheathing my dick with her sweet heat. "Oh, fuck yes," I gasp. "Ride me, honey."

She moans into my mouth as her hips begin to move.

I try to take in every movement, every second. I don't want to forget anything about this moment. The way her lips taste mine as we kiss, or the breathy little sounds she's making as she slides against me.

With a pounding heart, I ease my body into her rhythm. When I lift my hips, she moans. When I stroke her breasts, she lets fly a breathy sob. "You're so beautiful," I whisper. "I'm the luckiest guy in the world tonight."

She looks at me with wonder in her eyes. And I need more, suddenly. I hold her close and roll onto my side, fucking her in short, purposeful strokes.

"Oh, Liam," she chants. "So good."

I roll us further until she's spread out underneath me like a goddess. Her generous breasts look like a feast to me, so I dip down and tongue one of her nipples, then suck it into my mouth. My hips pick up the pace.

Sadie moans. "Don't. Stop."

Oh boy. I'm living out my fantasy right now. But every guy knows that "don't stop" means the stakes are high. So naturally I feel a tightness in my balls, letting me know I'm approaching the point of no return.

I clench every muscle in my body to try to stave it off. I think about my teacher. I think of the periodic table of elements. I think about thermonuclear war.

No! A bomb going off is not the image I need right now. "Oh, fuck," I gasp. "*Honey.*" I close my eyes and focus on her.

Then I hear it—a sharp intake of breath. And then another one. I open my eyes just in time to see a look of pure bliss cross her face.

And then it's all over for me but the moaning and the shaking and the sweet nothings that fall from my lips as I unload my entire soul inside her sweet body.

"Thank you," she whispers as I collapse beside her. "I needed that so badly."

"Garrummmph," I agree. But I'm not capable of forming actual words. I just hold on to her beautiful curves and kiss everything I can reach. Her hairline. Her nose. Everything.

11 OH HONEY.

Sadie

TWO WEEKS, now. Two weeks of Therapist By Day, Sex Goddess By Night. (And mom twenty-four/seven.)

I'm not saying I'm a sex goddess, exactly, but Liam certainly makes me feel like one. Night after night, he seduces me with smiles and kisses that make me feel like I'm twenty again and not *cough-cough* thirty-five.

And, wonder of wonders, now we're going to have a whole weekend together alone.

It's Decker's weekend with the girls. He used to take them every other weekend, but now because of his "hectic schedule" it's only once a month. He's the one missing out. But I'm still jazzed up for just a short break from being a mom.

For forty-eight hours I'm going to be just a woman.

And Liam has a surprise for me. I know this because he literally said "I have a surprise for you." It involves the weekend. I'm not even sure where we're going. When I asked what to pack, he said it didn't matter so long as I brought along that silk robe he likes me in.

So I packed one of everything. And then I did the same for my girls.

At home after work, I'm trying to be Zen about handing off the girls to Decker and his girlfriend. I liked the girl fine as our nanny. She seemed attentive. And Decker certainly needs help handling the twins.

See? I can do this. I'm as calm as a breezeless summer day. And I can stay that way, so long as she doesn't smirk at me with that smug little smile as she leads my girls away from me.

Yikes.

Honestly, handing them over to anyone for the weekend is hard. Even their father. I just have to trust that Decker has our girls' best interest at heart. I'm not sure I can ever trust him again, though. I did before, and look how that turned out?

Also, I'm worried about the girls getting too attached to The Nanny. She has an actual name, but I don't want to speak it. Like Voldemort. If I don't say it aloud, it can't hurt me.

So where the heck are they, anyway? He was supposed to be here at four, and I'm on a schedule. Liam and I have taken great pains that the girls only see him at daycare, and not at our home. I don't want them to start relying on him when he's only a temporary fling.

Liam has said he'd be happy to hang out with the girls and me together. But I haven't taken him up on it. They *love* Liam, and that's the whole problem. I don't want him to become a fixture in their home when I can feel in my gut that our fling will be short.

I check my watch. Again. Decker should be here by now, and he isn't. I've packed two enormous bags for the girls stuffed with everything they might possibly need. Extra bedding, spare pacifier, diapers, wipes, the ever present Neosporin, yogurt snacks, and outfits for every season.

I may have overdone it. But Michigan weather can be awfully unpredictable.

And Liam will be here to pick me up in less than an hour. I

planned for some alone time after the girls leave, so that I can take a shower and shave all the parts that will be visible or touchable to Liam, which means basically *all the parts*.

I can't show up for our date weekend with Chewbacca legs. I just can't.

Right now, Liam is probably in the shower, too, water sluicing over his toned muscles, stroking himself while he thinks about our weekend activities...

At least I hope he is.

The next time I check my watch, Decker is officially fifteen minutes late. My prep time is down to forty-five minutes. That's okay. I can do a quick shave. A quick moisturize. I've got plenty of time. "Girls!" I call. "Who needs a drink?"

———

Half an hour later, I'm about ready to lose my shit. Decker promised he'd be here at four p.m. It's almost five. By 5:30, the girls are going to start clamoring for dinner. If he doesn't feed them, they'll be in full meltdown mode by 5:31 and all hell will break loose. Kate has developed the peculiar penchant for climbing doorways and biting things. Usually she bites a toy, but I could see her gnawing on Decker's leg if he isn't careful.

That's actually tempting. Maybe I shouldn't try to fix everything. Let him experience the twins in their full meltdown glory.

Gah!

Where the fuck is Decker? What if he doesn't show up at all? I'll have to cancel my sexy weekend with Liam, and I really want this. I need it. It's been ages since I've had some time for me. I want my time with my lover man and wherever it is that we're going and I want to drink a cocktail without worrying about it and I want to sleep in, please, for just once, I want to sleep in and...

There's a knock on the door. It's still a little weird that Decker would knock. This used to be his house and...

Wait a minute. That's a knock at the back door, not the front. It's not Decker at all. I look at my watch. 4:58! That knock is Liam.

I'm not ready for Decker to meet Liam. It's too soon for that. It shouldn't happen at all because Liam and I are just a fling and...

I open the back door. Liam is showered and shaved, and he is holding a bouquet of wildflowers. My heart begins to quiver at the sight of him. My heart, plus a few other parts. "Hi," I say, and my voice is a little breathy.

"Hi," he says, a little breathy too. "Do you think you could open the screen door and actually let me in?"

What I should say is "Oh sure!" What I actually say is "Oh. No!" Because that's when I hear the doorbell ring. At the front of the house. And that *is* Decker.

The girls erupt into shouts and cheers. They're jumping up and down. If they see Liam and their dad at the same time...I just don't know what will happen.

"Just a sec!" I say and then I close the actual door and not just the screen part on Liam. I'm sure those wildflowers instantly droop.

I'm a bad person. I'm a bad, bad person.

"Hey, Sadie? SADIE?" I hear Decker call, and my quivering loins stop quivering and retreat into my body, if that's a thing. Yep. It's a thing.

"Daddy! Daddy!" The girls shriek. I hear them open the door and can actually feel Decker enter my space. My Space. This is mine. And he does not belong here. Does he not see the pillows? They're supposed to be a Decker retardant. Stay back!! Out, vampire!

Deep breaths, my inner therapist reminds me.

Why didn't you prescribe me some valium, I ask her.

I run to the front of the house just in time to see a woman in a slinky dress bending down and offering her hand to Amy and then Kate. This is not The Nanny. This is someone else. Someone new. Someone who is actually not much younger than I am.

But there's one crucial difference. This woman is sleek and put together and...oh no. Kate has her helmet on and before I can stop her, she charges right for the woman, bringing her down in a perfect tackle worthy of any Sunday Night Football broadcast.

Inwardly, I cheer.

The woman sprawls across my floor, her sleek long legs going at weird angles. Decker helps her up before I can do anything. But then he says "For Chrissakes, Sadie, what are you teaching the girls?"

I'm so stunned I can't even speak. What am I teaching the girls? Stranger Danger! Of course. And who is this woman?

"Here, Honey, let me help you," Decker says, his voice all sweet. He actually calls her honey. "Honey, you okay?"

Then he does it again. What. The. Fuck.

She laughs, but it's not a real laugh. "I'm fine. Fine. They are just..." Slight pause. "Charming."

She extends her hand and she's walking toward me. Her nails are really long and pointy. Maybe she's going to gouge me. I wonder if Liam is watching through the window. Hopefully he'll call 911 if this woman attacks. But no, she wants a handshake. So I tentatively take her hand. It's a limp handshake. It gives me the willies.

"I'm Honey," she says. "So happy to meet you."

Oh! Her name is actually Honey. The sugar in her voice and name make me want to pass out.

Suddenly, I don't want Decker to have the girls. I'll cancel my plans with Liam. I'll get Ash and Braht to babysit and I'll just sneak over to his house for a little midnight nookie, and then come back and the girls will never know. Because I do not know this woman. This stranger. And how could Decker bring a new woman into the girls' lives? I swear to God, it was only last week that he was with The Nanny. Isn't he even the least bit discerning? Doesn't he care?

Decker grabs the girls' gear, eyeing the duffel bag like it's offended him. "Really, Sadie? It's only for one night. I'd think a backpack would suffice."

There's so much wrong with that statement that I just want to wallop him with the bag. It takes everything I have to remain calm. I remind myself that I want the girls to have a healthy relationship with their father. I want him to be present in their lives. The girls need their father too. But I also need a break. "It's for the *weekend*. You're not dropping them off until Sunday evening."

"Yeah, but Honey and I have decided to go to a wine tasting and..."

My blood is boiling so intensely that I think my skin might melt off. I can't believe we have to have this conversation. Again! But I can't show the girls how mad I am. Also, I want this over with quickly because I've left Liam in the back of my house and forced him to hide.

"Decker," I say in my calmest voice. "The girls are ready for a great weekend with you," I say. "According to the agreement, you have forty-eight hours. And I've made plans." My inner therapist is doing a slow clap. It's hard to have boundaries. It's hard to deal with Decker at all.

Honey comes to the rescue. "Oh, it's *fine*. It was just an *idea*. We can have them for the *weekend*. Maybe we can get a *puppy*." The way she *talks*, makes me want to *kick* things. And you don't offer a puppy to toddlers. EVER.

The girls are beyond freaking out. Kate is spinning in circles and Amy is sucking so furiously on her pacifier that she and Piggypoo are going to lift off into the atmosphere.

But this is not my problem.

I may want to control everything, but I can't.

"Let me help you to the car," I offer weakly, feeling my cheeks flush and my eyes threaten to tear up. I will be strong for the girls. This is the new normal. I can do this.

"Not necessary," Honey says. "We've got this, don't we, babe?"

"Sure," Decker smirks.

Sure he does.

"Okay," I say. I hug and kiss the girls and watch Honey take their hands and Decker take the bags. He's brought his stupid old convertible, but I can see he at least put the car seats in the back so, fine. Okay. I watch them pull away, feeling like a little piece of my heart is going on vacation. I can actually feel it leaving my body.

A single thought slingshots me back into action. Liam!

———

Liam

Now, you'd think I'd be storming mad and just stomp off into the distance. I mean, first she slams the door in my face, and then she seemingly forgets about me. But it's all good. Really. It is.

I can tell what happened. Decker was late.

And I can also hear everything that's happening now. I'm not above a little eavesdropping. I cringe at the name Honey. And my face scrunches at the tone of voice Decker uses when he talks to Sadie. What a patronizing anus. And then there's the mention of puppies and it takes everything in me not to go in there right now and rescue Sadie and the girls.

Maybe I won't have to. Maybe we should just cancel our plans and...

I listen.

She's standing up to him. She's being firm. She could be a lot firmer, but this is a start. *Good for you*, I want to tell her. I want to high-five her. And then later, I want to push her up against a wall and lick her all over.

Maybe I'll have the chance.

The back door suddenly opens.

"I am so sorry!" she says. "Come in! Come in! I'm so so so sorry! I panicked!"

"It's okay, Sadie. Really. But maybe just don't make a habit of that?" I hand her the flowers.

"Oh! They're in a pot!" she says, and I'm a little proud of myself here. I wanted to bring her flowers, but by the time she gets back from our weekend, they'd be dead. Hence, it's a small pot for her patio.

She sets the flowers on the counter and turns to me. I slide my arms around her and pull her to me—close, firm—and just kiss her. I kiss her because she's nervous and I want to calm her down, but I also kiss her because it's a physical need. I'm drawn to her. She sighs into me and only then do I release her.

"Let's get out of here," I say.

———

"When do I get to find out where we're going?" Sadie asks as I head west on the highway.

"I'll tell you now." There's no point in making too big a deal out of it. I don't want to build it up too much in case Sadie hates my choice. "We're going to my family's obnoxious home on Lake Macatawa. My parents bought the place about five years ago."

Sadie stiffens beside me, and I realize I forgot to mention one other important fact.

"We'll be the only ones there. We'll have every obnoxious square foot to ourselves."

"Oh." She relaxes. "Wow. Cool."

It shouldn't bother me that Sadie doesn't want to see my parents. I mean—she's already met them. When she babysat us, my parents barely showed their faces. She knows they're tools. Hell, *I* don't even want to meet them. But it bums me out that we'll never have an awkward *meet the parents* dinner with either of our families. Because Sadie is just in this for the sex.

As far as she knows, so am I. But I've been in love with her since I was fourteen. I know I'm not allowed to say so. Sadie would hightail it out of my life faster than you can say *relationship PTSD*.

I prefer to think of her reluctance to consider me a boyfriend has more to do with her divorce than her thinking I'm too young for her. But I'm probably fooling myself.

"What makes the house obnoxious, exactly?" she asks as I slow down to take our exit.

"You'll see. The architect had a king-sized ego. It's too big and too fancy for a lake house. Luckily it's the kind of place you can disdain and enjoy at the same time. That's what we're going to do." I eye the dashboard clock. "And we're going straight there because I have a couple of deliveries coming at six-fifteen."

"What's being delivered?"

"Dinner, for starters. Tomorrow night we can go out, but tonight I thought you'd just want to relax."

"That is so nice of you! By 'relax,' did you mean 'strip me naked'?"

"Oh, the naked will happen." I give her the side eye. "But first you are going to be so relaxed you won't be able to feel your face. I have a surprise for you."

"A surprise that makes me unable to feel my face? You're going to...roofie me?"

I snort. "Not exactly. Fifteen minutes from now all will be revealed."

———

Sadie

When Liam pulls into a circular driveway, my first thought is that we've stopped outside a hotel. But no. It's one very large house.

Liam parks his car right in front of the gleaming double wooden doors and gets out. He pulls my duffel bag out of the trunk and looks up at the house. From his pocket he pulls a key fob. When he pushes a button, the double doors open slowly.

"That's very Disney World," I say, climbing out of the car.

"It's something," he sighs. "Come on. I'll show you the house."

We enter the sprawling, light-filled foyer of an enormous contemporary home. Beyond the foyer I can see the main living area, with its floor-to-ceiling windows and double-height ceiling. There are one-hundred-and-eighty degree views out onto a private fenced-in lawn, a swimming pool, and a dock on the lake.

The view is impressive, but the interior space looks about as warm and personal as a chic Miami Beach hotel lobby. "This is... pretty great," I say, which is true.

"If you like ostentatious echo chambers," he says with a grin. "My room isn't so bad though. It's in the west wing."

This house has actual wings. Jesus. I follow Liam down a broad hallway hung with artwork. The last room on the left is his. It's large, but not echoing. There's a sisal carpet on the floor, a set of fishing poles on hooks on the wall, and several comfortable pillows on the bed.

Liam doesn't hate pillows. I think he's my spirit animal.

"This is nice," I say, meaning it.

"Thanks, babe." He gives me a quick hug. "Listen, I booked a massage for you. So if you don't want a guy named Sven rubbing oil into all of your muscles, now would be the right moment to say so."

"A massage?" I squeak. "Well, only if his name is really Sven."

Liam laughs, low and throaty.

"Honestly, that's the best gift ever. It's been eons since I had a massage. Since before I was pregnant with Kate and Amy."

His blue eyes are smiling at me. "Really?"

"Really. I love it."

He picks me up and kisses me. And I like it a whole lot.

———

My massage will take place in the "spa room" of the McAllister family mansion. It's a sunlit space with a water feature on the wall and an ostentatiously healthy bamboo plant. I wonder who cleans this place, and who waters the bamboo. I'm pretty sure it's neither Mr. nor Mrs. McAllister.

Sven turns out to be a nice Korean-American guy from Grand Rapids. "I get more jobs as Sven, but my real name is Kevin," he explains. "Now tell me about your trouble areas."

"My trouble areas are that my ex-husband has my two-year-old twins for an entire weekend, along with his new girlfriend named Honey."

Kevin/Sven cringes. "That sounds rough, but I meant to ask if any particular muscles are troubling you."

"Ah. My shoulders are tight."

"Let's fix that," he says. "Remove as much clothing as you're comfortable with and cover yourself with the sheet. I'll warm up my oil and be back in five," he says.

When he returns to the room, I feel self-conscious on that table for about seven seconds. But then I discover that he has magically strong hands. He starts on my upper back and spends a nice long time turning my shoulder muscles to putty. By the time he's massaged my arms and my lower legs, I'm too blissed out to care that he spends a couple of businesslike minutes on my gluteus maximus.

I also don't care that my gluteus maximus is more maximal

than it used to be. I don't care about a single thing in the world, in fact.

When Kevin is done with me, I actually have to wipe drool off the corner of my mouth to thank him for his services. "That was everything," I slur. "Is there anything you need from me?"

"Not a thing, it's all covered," he says. "You just relax, and I'll show myself out."

Then I nearly fall asleep on the table. I feel like a cooked noodle. Every muscle is relaxed, and my body feels supple and... Horny. All that rubbing has awoken every nerve ending in my body, because they all know that Liam is one or two excessively large rooms away.

For another five minutes I lie there thinking happy thoughts about him. Then I peel myself off the table and pull on a fluffy white robe that's been left for me.

Liam is a god, and I'm in paradise. (So long as your version of paradise is one constructed by rich white conservatives who golf and spa.)

I shuffle out into the giant, light-filled living room, with its stunning windows that look out on the lake, which is sparkling in the slanting late afternoon sun. There sits Liam on the L-shaped sofa. He's holding a lap desk covered with papers, and frowning down at some notes he's writing.

When he looks up, I see reading glasses perched on his nose. Liam McAllister is hot and nerdy and smiley and serious and a hundred other things, all at once. My heart goes pitter-patter just looking at him. "Hey," he says softly. "Feeling good?"

"I feel *great*," I admit. "Oily, but amazing. I should shower."

He licks his lips. "What if you didn't?"

"But I'm..." I trace a hand across my chest where it's exposed above the V of the robe. "Slick."

He stands up, dumping papers everywhere. "What if slick is a big turn-on?"

"Oh." My vagina quivers. "Is it?"

He stalks toward me. "My hands sliding all over your body? Doesn't that sound good to you?"

I gulp.

"Or, wait." There's a dirty gleam in his eye. "We could shower together. Swear to God I have about a hundred ideas for fucking you. I can't even choose."

I feel a full-body shiver when the word *fuck* comes out of Liam's mouth. It's not a word I've ever liked before, and I never use it myself. And Decker was too buttoned up to ever talk dirty.

God help me but younger men make me insane. Particularly this one.

"Follow me," he says, his voice husky. He takes my hand and leads me down the hallway, into a museum gallery. Okay, no. It's actually a bathroom. But it's so large you could hang Monet's *Water Lilies* in here. Glittering glass tiles sparkle on all four over-sized walls, like so many little jewels.

Liam drops my hand so he can operate a touch screen on the wall. As soon as he does, water springs forth on the opposite wall, spouting from three—no, four—different shower heads clustered together.

"You won't be needing this," Liam says, pushing my robe off my shoulders. He kicks it toward a laundry hamper in the corner.

I'm naked with Liam again, my subconscious prods. *Maybe this time he'll notice that I'm not twenty-five and I have stretch marks.*

"Unbutton my shirt," he says instead. And his hot gaze is trained right on my breasts, which he's cupping in his hands, like a pirate clutching new treasure. "Come on, sexy," he prompts with a smile. "Make it snappy."

My heart jumps at the command. With clumsy fingers, I reach up to do what he asks. Or I try, anyway. But my dexterity goes a little haywire as he strokes his thumbs across my nipples and leans down to take my mouth in a kiss.

"Faster," he says against my lips. "I need you."

All of a sudden I *feel* twenty-five. As Liam kicks off his shorts and underwear and steers me underneath the warm spray of multiple shower heads, I'm someone I haven't been in a long time —a naughty party girl on spring break. I watch rivulets of water run down Liam's pecs as he reaches for a bottle and squirts something into his hand.

He lathers his hands together and then smooths soap bubbles across my breasts. Strong hands pass over my arms and shoulders. Then he pulls me against his body so he can stroke across my back and bottom. He grabs another squirt of shampoo and rubs it into my hair. And I'm cradled against him like a precious thing.

Everything is soapy, wet bliss. I look down and see his erection, trapped between our bodies. By now I've had multiple viewings of a naked, turned-on Liam, and he never ceases to amaze me. His muscular, golden body flips all my switches.

So I drop to my knees right there in the shower.

"Oh, fuck yes," Liam groans as I run my tongue up his shaft. And when I open my mouth and take him inside, he sighs my name. "*Sadie.*" It sounds like a prayer.

———

Shortly afterwards, we're lying on his bed, naked, our wet hair dripping on the pillow. His hands run over my damp skin as we kiss. "You are spectacular," he whispers. "But I wasn't planning on that. I only need fifteen minutes or so, and the show can go on." He slides a hand down between my legs and I have to bite my lip to keep from moaning.

All the sex we've been having has changed me into a super-sexual being. Maybe he's a sex god. Maybe it's the two-year dry spell. All I know is that every time Liam touches me I turn into a panting crazy person.

Liam groans again as he touches me. He heartily approves of my response to him. "Forget fifteen minutes," he says. "I only need five." He grips his burgeoning erection and gives himself a slow stroke.

I watch him and lick my lips.

"See something you like? How do you want the cock, honey?"

I bury my smile in his neck. "I can't do dirty talk. I just can't. I try to use anatomically correct words."

"Why?" He strokes himself again and I have to clench my thighs together. My reluctance to talk about sex sure doesn't translate into a reluctance to do it.

"Well, so I don't sound crude."

He smiles. "Okay, fine. But when we're naked, I'm thinking very crude thoughts about you. But I could try to be more anatomically correct."

"You don't have to," I say, and then blush furiously.

"Let's experiment," he says, reaching out to stroke a hand down my very naked body. "Here's how it is with me. When I see your breasts, my blood flows toward my pelvis, swelling my penis to medically significant proportions."

I giggle in spite of myself.

"This causes primary and secondary arousal reactions. My heart rate increases, especially if you're touching yourself, or touching me. My testicles become tighter. And I experience a sudden release of..." He leans over and whispers in my ear. "*Oxytocin,* baby."

I *die*. But he's not done.

"You'll feel it, too," he continues. "When I rub my hand all over my glans," he does this very thing as he rolls a condom down his length. "...Your mouth will water. Your nipples will experience increased blood flow. Your breasts might swell. When I touch your labia and your clitoris, nerve endings will send a signal to your brain with a message."

"What message?" I gasp as his thick fingers swirl between my legs.

"The cock wants the pussy. Duh."

He climbs on top of me as I draw his smile closer to mine. He smells of expensive shampoo and naked man. And then he slides inside me and I'm not smiling anymore. I'm too lost in the heat and the stretch as my body accommodates the hottest, most amazing man I've ever known in my life.

He makes love to me...No he *fucks* me in long, slow strokes, until I lose my mind.

12 SAMOSAS AT SUNSET

Liam

WE LIE on my bed for a long time afterward. I can hear the call of seagulls and the distant sound of waves lapping against the lakeshore.

Sex with Sadie always burns up all the stresses in my life. When I'm inside her, it's like being home in the best kind of way. It's like feeling a missing piece of myself click into place.

And it's not just when we're having sex. Just being around her is enough to make me feel...whole. This has never happened to me before, and I have to admit that it scares me a little.

Because I know I will probably lose her, and I know it will hurt.

True story—I've always had a thing for older women. I blame my longstanding Sadie fascination. My last girlfriend was thirty-six. She really wasn't interested in a long-term commitment. She was looking for a boy toy, and I was happy to play that role. We eventually got tired of each other and said goodbye. No big loss. We shared a toast to good times and moved on.

But as I listen to Sadie's heartbeat slow down, I know I'm

starting to feel a tug. I spent her massage hour going over the specs of the study I'll be conducting this fall. A few months from now I'll be in Edinburgh or maybe Rome. Six months ago, that's what I thought I wanted.

But now I'm not so sure. I dread leaving Sadie. If I wasn't leaving, I feel like we'd have a chance for our fling to grow into something much more.

She's not there yet. I know this. She doesn't see the potential. I'm afraid if I take off for Europe, she never will.

These are my thoughts as Sadie stretches and yawns. Reluctantly I release her, and she slides off the bed. I ogle her naked body as she unzips her duffel bag and pulls out a sundress, which she slips over her head.

There's nothing under that dress, fourteen-year-old Liam points out. *We can see the outline of her beautiful body!*

He's right. I'm tempted to ask her to stand on the dock while I prep dinner so I can just watch the sun set behind her. But that would be a little awkward, and we'll have even more fun if we're cooking together.

"It's chow time," I say, sitting up. "Dinner was delivered. Shall we put it together?"

"Of course." Sadie smiles at me, and it's like someone is plucking on my heartstrings.

Since when am I such a sap? Oh, right. Since the moment I kissed her after our trek to the park. I haven't really been the same since.

I take her hand and lead her into my parents' ridiculous kitchen. I'm the only one who ever cooks in here, I swear. My parents dine out for ten meals a week. No lie.

"Whoa," Sadie says when she opens the refrigerator. "You have a whole grocery store of ingredients here," she says. "I thought you were just going to keep it simple. I thought you were ordering in."

"I did order in," I say. "I ordered the groceries. Emil's Vineyard delivers." I'm a little smug about this, because I have no doubt that if Sadie doesn't already love me just a little bit, she will after dinner. "Plus, cooking relaxes me."

We've got the lake in front of us, a sunset in an hour or so. First things first. I open up a bottle of wine and pour two glasses. "You want to be my sous chef?" I ask.

"Sure. What are we having?"

"Potato and pea samosas and grilled masala white fish. And rice."

Sadie frowns. "That sounds...complicated. I'm rusty in the kitchen. At my house lately, 'cooking' means just cutting food into pieces a two-year-old can't choke on."

"Don't worry. This stuff is easy. I'll show you. And I already made the samosa dough." It was the first thing I did while Sadie was getting her massage.

"Okay..." she says.

"Come here," I say. Not because I want to show her how to cook, I just want to wrap my arms around her and breathe her into me. After a bit, I let go. "First, we roll out the dough and then stuff the samosas. We can fry or bake them. And the fish...we just stuff it, slather on some marinade, and it'll go on the grill."

She looks at me like she doesn't quite believe me. "It's easy," I say as I attach the pasta maker to the counter. The roller works great for samosas. I'm in my zone right now. "Grab my phone and choose some music. Then I'll show you how to roll these out. You roll, I'll stuff," I say.

She laughs. "Ooh baby."

We work together, making more samosas than we can possibly eat. We fall into a quiet rhythm together. I like it way too much. We wash our hands and she fills the rice cooker with rice and water without my asking. I score the fish and begin to stuff it with lemon, fresh coriander, and a few chilis.

"How'd you learn how to do all of this?" she asks.

"What, cook?"

"Yeah, cook. I mean I can prepare basic recipes, but this feels like a whole new level. This is like cooking show genius happening."

I blush like a smitten teenager. "It's hardly genius level. I was shooting for Super Romantic and Somewhat Impressive. But I learned to cook because of my parents."

"Oh, were they trained at Le Cordon Bleu or something?"

"No, the opposite." I rub coriander into the white fish. Once it's slathered in sauce and then grilled to flaky perfection? Yum. It's enough to get me a little turned on. "That summer you spent with us—did you see them cook anything?"

"No."

"Right. They order in or have the cook do it." It's so embarrassing. "My parents think all labor is beneath them. I think I learned to cook just to spite them. Or at least to balance that out."

"Feeding themselves is beneath them?"

"Sure. And so is parenting." I try to make this sound light-hearted, but she can probably see through me. "You remember. A new nanny every few months. I'm positive that's what led me to study childcare and psychology. And to Indian spices." I smile at her.

Sadie puts a hand lightly in the center of my back, letting me know she's listening.

The rice starts to bubble. The sliding glass doors are wide open, and there's a breeze kicking up. Life is great, but I can't seem to stop talking about my screwy family. It's not something I usually discuss with women. Nobody wants to hear the rich guy complain.

But Sadie gets me. She always has.

"Hey, did you see that my dad is running for circuit court judge?"

"Sure. There are signs in some of the yards in our neighborhood." She tops up our glasses of wine.

"I think it's the perfect job for him, since he loves to judge people." My siblings and I spent our childhoods trying to be good enough for him. The other three all have jobs that he's proud of. "I'm the black sheep, can you believe that? I'm an embarrassment to the family. They don't put me on the Christmas card anymore."

"Why the hell not? That's so sad!"

"Well, my attitude doesn't help. The others show up in a suit. I always wear a bad Christmas sweater. I have a collection of those."

Her smile is wicked. "I need to see that."

You'll just have to wait for Christmas, I almost say, but then I remember. By Christmas, I'll be in Edinburgh, or Italy, or California. Sadie and the girls will open presents without me.

This idea feels impossibly crushing, and in spite of the fine weather and even finer company, I feel my soul sag.

Good thing the fish is ready for the grill. "Let's go outside, okay?"

"Let's." I get another warm smile.

Man, I like this Sadie. I like all the Sadies, but *this* Sadie, when she's so fully relaxed and comfortable, it's such a turn-on. I kiss her once before heading back out to the deck. She tastes like crisp wine and a hint of spice. She tastes like everything I've ever wanted.

———

Sadie

I cannot quite put into words how divine this dinner is. The fish is spicy and flaky and tastes of summer. The samosas are crisp on the outside and fluffy in the center. Liam whips up some raita, and there are chutneys for dipping.

I'm perfectly content. Seriously. I don't know how long it's been since I've been this relaxed. I have my occasional nights out with the girlfriends, but those are only a few hours. I've been here all evening with Liam and we have the weekend stretching out in front of us.

After dinner, he reads some more journal articles. I read, too. A book. An actual book. And I don't know how long it's been since I've had the time or energy to focus on reading without being interrupted by the girls, or Decker, or life in general. It's so relaxing to lounge outside. The lake laps gently before us. The only other sound is the gentle typing of Liam's fingers on his laptop as he scrolls through the academic research.

When I look up from my book, I study Liam. He's wearing shorts and an open shirt. His hair is messy and his reading glasses make him look professorial. My pulse kicks up. And just like that, I've lost focus on the book.

Liam has his bare feet stretched out on a lawn chair, so I lift them up, sit down in their place, and then rest his feet in my lap. I begin to rub slow circles into the sole of one foot. Liam has great feet. Not everyone does, and I have the urge to kiss them.

Is my libido unlocked, or what?

I rub his foot a little more firmly, and Liam groans.

It's an excellent groan.

"You're distracting me," he says, the tone suggesting maybe he wants me to keep distracting him.

"Put that computer down and let me distract you some more."

"So tempting, but let me just finish this page. Then we can watch the sunset and..."

"...And get naked and make love on this here patio furniture?"

"It's quality furniture," he says. "It can totally support us." I squeeze his foot. He smirks.

"Still reading about cognitive intransigence?" Fine. So I looked over his shoulder a couple of times. Sue me.

"Nope." He frowns over the laptop. "I'm looking over the list of child development centers where my study is happening."

My hands forget to rub Liam's foot. "Did they notify you? Do you know where you're going to be?"

Slowly, he shakes his head. "Still nothing. But they'll tell me sometime in the next two weeks."

That is really, really soon. "Where do you think it will be?"

"Not sure," he says. "I was just reading about their location in Germany."

"Germany, Michigan?" I ask hopefully.

He laughs. "Germany, *Germany*. Lederhosen and sausage and beer halls. There's a child development center there doing some good work."

I want to laugh but it sort of gets stuck in my throat. Germany? That's so far. And foreign. "Won't the children speak German?" I ask. "How could you even work there?"

"It wouldn't matter," he tells me. "Because we're evaluating the children's motor skills after they learn something from a volunteer or from a video."

"Oh," I say slowly. *Germany*. He's also applying to something in Scotland, and Italy, I think. After a few short months, I might not see him again.

The idea makes me mentally hyperventilate. Okay, that's not really a thing. But I'm definitely panicked. Because I know I'm getting too attached to him. Liam was supposed to be my boy toy. A distraction. This is all just sex and fun.

Just like that, my eyes fill with tears.

"I need some more wine," I lie and make a hasty retreat into the kitchen and then the bathroom. Why are my emotions so out of sync with reality? I'm a single mom who is six years older than him. He's a sexy bachelor who has his whole future ahead of him.

I'm the cougar. He's the snack.

So why am I feeling teary? Liam would look sexy in lederhosen, and I won't get a chance to see it.

I'm not ready for this to end. Not yet.

———

Liam

Sadie takes a while to bring out another bottle of wine, but it's just enough time for me to brood. Our time together is limited. I'll have another month and a half at the daycare center, then I'll have a couple of months for research prep before continuing my fellowship overseas.

Six months from now I'll be somewhere far away, even if I'm not sure where. Yet six months ago, I had my heart set on traveling abroad. Suddenly I hate that idea.

"Come here," I say as soon as Sadie appears.

She's carrying two glasses of wine. It's our favorite Australian white. Fruity. Crisp. Delicious. Perfect for a warm night. She hands me the glass and I set it down on the side table. "Come here," I repeat and give her a little tug.

I spread my legs and she sits down on the lounge chair with me. She leans back against my chest, and I wrap my arms around her. The sun is just starting to set in streaks of red and orange. There are layers of purple and blue above the horizon, over the lake.

"You can actually hear the sun sink below the horizon," I say.

"You cannot!" She laughs and sips her wine. She hands me the glass and I take a sip too.

"You can. Watch."

And we do. We just sit like that, my arms around her, her leaning into me and watch the sun sink and the world darken. Just when the last of it disappears, I make a pop sound and she giggles.

"Huh," she says, playing along. "I never noticed that before."

"Pretty amazing," I say. "Right?"

There's a pause and then she says. "You *are* pretty amazing."

Then I can't wait anymore. I move her hair away from her neck and slowly kiss the curve of her until she can't take it anymore and she turns around and kisses me.

"About getting naked out here and..."

"Fucking al fresco?" I ask.

"Yeah," she kisses me again.

"I totally meant it," I say.

And then we don't say another word.

———

On the way home on Sunday, I'm still feeling the weekend glow. "What are you going to do with the rest of your evening?" I ask her.

"Hug my girls," she says immediately. "And probably wean them off the sugar high they'll be on from whatever lazy treats their father gave them. You?"

"I'll probably run five or ten miles and go to the climbing gym."

"I'm tired just thinking about that."

"No." He shakes his head. "You're tired because I tired you *out*." I reach over and palm her thigh. Waking up next to Sadie this morning was amazing, and not just because of the sleepy, Sunday morning sex. It was lovely to lie there and doze and not worry that I'll accidentally fall asleep in her bed.

Sneaking out at midnight is kind of a buzzkill. "Hey, can I ask you something?"

"Of course." She lays her hand atop mine.

"At my climbing gym there's a kids' wall. I think Kate would really like it. We're always telling her she can't climb things. Wouldn't it be super fun to put a harness on her and say, 'Have at it, you little monkey'?" The idea makes me grin. "Let's all go there together next weekend. I'd offer to take them myself, but there's a one-to-one rule for parents and caregivers."

Sadie is silent for a moment. Then she breaks my heart. "We can't, Liam. It's not a good idea."

Okay.

Well.

Wow.

I wasn't expecting to be shot down quite so fast. "It's not a sleepover, Sadie. Just an hour at a gym."

Her fingers massage mine, but I don't like what she says next. "You're leaving in a few months. Even if you don't know where yet, it's going to happen. I don't want them to get used to you."

"They're *already* used to me. I see them for most of their waking hours, Monday through Friday."

When Sadie withdraws her hand, I know I've fucked up. It was the wrong thing to say, because it sounds like I'm making a judgement about where the twins spend their week. "Shit," I say immediately. "I didn't mean it like a criticism."

"I know," she says.

But she's quiet for the rest of the ride home. And I feel my happy glow slipping away.

13 EVERGREEN SPRINGS. GROSS.

Liam

SURE ENOUGH, my happy glow fades to a dull silver. A dim tarnish?

Whatever.

I'm too grumpy to get the analogy right. And when my happiness leaves, it's replaced by a numbness that I can't seem to fight off. I'd done it—I'd set up the perfect weekend. And then I wrecked it by pushing Sadie into acknowledging the truth. And by having too many feelings.

I still have them, too. And I don't know how to stop.

When Monday morning rolls around, I eye the wall clock in the daycare, knowing Sadie will soon arrive. When she brings in the girls for drop-off, I avoid her by attending to some very important paperwork.

Yes, it's cowardly. But I don't want her to notice that I'm hurting. I care about her a great deal, and yet I'm just a boy toy to her. And she's put herself firmly in the cougar category, when it's not like that at all. At least not for me.

My sulkiness lasts all day. I'm stuck on the hamster wheel of my own thoughts. By the time five o'clock arrives, I'm actually relieved to have family plans. Usually, "relieved" and "family plans" are not words I put together in a sentence. But tonight I'm only seeing my siblings, and not those robots we refer to as our parents. I love my siblings. They've got me right in the feels.

But our parents? Man, our parents. Both of them are attorneys —McAllister Esq. & McAllister Esq, Attorneys at Law. They're finally splitting up. Not their marriage, but their partnership in the firm. Dad is running for a judgeship. The election is this November, and so my brothers and sister and I are currently trying to find the right place for his surprise victory party.

At six-thirty, I pull up to the Evergreen Springs Golf Club. Evergreen Springs sounds more like a cemetery than a fancy club, but it's exactly the sort of stuffy establishment that my father loves. Aiden, Connor, and Cassidy are waiting for me outside the door of the lodge. As soon as I reach them, I'm surrounded. "Where were you?" a brother demands. "You're five minutes late! That is so unlike you," Cassidy insists.

Then Aiden, younger than me by five years, jokes, "Pops is getting forgetful in his old age." And we all laugh, even though it's not very funny. When they were young, I was the one they relied on, and was often in charge when the nanny wasn't around or our parents were late, which was always.

Cassidy, the youngest, gives me a big hug, then Aiden and Connor join in. We're just a big ball of sappy family love.

Forgive us. We're dorky that way.

"Okay, okay!" I say. "Break it up! Do you think we could just get this over with?"

"Jeez, grumpy much?" asks Connor. Connor is an attorney now, too. He'll be taking over for dad when he wins the judgeship. *If* he wins. Aiden is in finance.

Cassidy is a legal scholar. That's her way of skirting the line of Dad's approval. She wanted to be an academic like me, but she chose the law as her area of expertise. I'm pretty sure my baby sister enjoys her work, but I've always wondered what she would have chosen if my dad weren't such a hardass about his kids' life choices.

And then there's me. The Manny. The respect I get from my parents? Not a lot. Mostly I don't care.

Mostly.

"I am grumpy," I agree.

"Duh," says Connor.

"Did you break up with another girlfriend?" asks Cassidy.

I hope not, I think, feeling glum all over again. But Sadie only wants me for sex, so a breakup is pretty much inevitable.

Yet I keep my mouth shut. This is neither the time nor the place.

"No comment," I say, opening the sort of heavy walnut door that's obligatory at an overpriced golf club, and then ushering my siblings inside.

"May I help you?" asks a woman behind a podium. Her bun is so severely gathered that it's stretching her face like Silly Putty. And she gives me a head-to-toe once-over that isn't the sort I'm used to. She isn't admiring my rock-climbing muscles. She's judging my shorts, flip-flops, and Sesame Street T-shirt. It features Cookie Monster with an empty cookie jar, reading "Straight Outta Cookies."

The receptionist doesn't like it, but I can assure you this shirt is very popular with the under-three set.

"We're here to see Sandy," I say, trying a friendly smile. "We have an appointment."

"Excuse me one moment," she says, trotting off toward the back. She gives us a dubious look over her shoulder as she goes.

"Jesus. We're not here to steal the silver," Connor mutters.

"There's probably a dress code," Cassidy whispers. "That's why I didn't change after work."

"Sorry," I tell my sister. "Didn't think about it." Cassidy is naturally respectful of authority. You sort of had to be to survive in our house growing up.

"You're the McAllister children?" a woman says, approaching us. "I'm Sandy."

We shake her hand dutifully, one by one. Sandy is nearing retirement age, and wearing clothes that fit her probably two decades ago. I can practically hear the buttons on her cardigan crying out from their struggles.

"Come this way," she says. "You'll be renting the Double Bogey room."

And now I'm annoyed all over again. Since we're just here to ask questions, it's awfully presumptuous of her to assume that we'll choose this place for Dad's party.

Or maybe it's not. The moment we walk through the doors into the Double Bogey room, my sister Cassidy whispers, "Oh God, really?"

And there stand my dad and mom in front of a picture window, admiring the perfect fantasy green hills and little golf flags outside.

My siblings fall in line behind me somehow, leaving me to greet our parents first. "Well this is a surprise," I say. Although, it isn't really. My dad is such a control freak that he wants to plan his own surprise party. I should have seen it coming.

"You're a few minutes late," dear old Dad says by way of a greeting. "And why aren't you properly attired?"

"Just came from my place of business," I say, patting the graphic on my chest. "Where I work, this *is* proper attire." Would my dad make playdough in a suit and Hermes tie?

Actually, he wouldn't make playdough at all.

"We've already gone ahead and approved everything," Mom says. "It's just perfect here!"

"But I thought this was a surprise party?" I say, just because I'm in a mood. I feel my brothers and sister tense up behind me.

You don't question my parents. Ever. "And who knows if you'll even win?" I say to my dad, further pushing my luck.

Seems like I'm just itching for a fight. The idea that my dad would lose his bid for the judgeship isn't even imaginable, not to him at least.

He gives me the Fearsome McAllister Frown. "Of *course* I'll be elected. It's a done deal. And we need this surprise party to look perfect."

"Everything *will* be perfect," Sandy says. "We're serving steak and scalloped potatoes. And nothing ever goes wrong at Evergreen Springs."

"It'll be picture perfect, I'm sure," I say drily.

I get elbowed in the ribs on both sides of my body at once.

Sandy launches into a long-winded description of the shrimp cocktail and the dessert menu. I can't focus on any of it, and I'm not sure why any of us are here.

God, I miss Sadie. If she were here, this would be so much more enjoyable. I could just quietly rub my hand up against her and...

"Dude," says Connor. "A little distance."

Whoops. I try to focus again.

"Jackets and ties," my father is saying. "Emerald green and navy blue would be acceptable. You will each have a plus one, and dance the second dance with your mother and me. A foxtrot."

Dancing? Fuck.

I hope Sadie sticks around with me long enough to come with me.

I am so in a funk right now.

Meh.

14 MY CRAZY PERSON VOICE

Sadie

MY GIRLS SURVIVED the weekend with their father. Afterwards, they're clingy and tired. But I'm still happy to see them.

On Monday it's back to the grind, although my psychology practice is quiet this week. Quite a few of my patients are away on vacation. When September comes, though, I know they'll be back. Psychologists see lots of demand in the fall when everyone is back to the stresses of school and work.

The summer lull means I get to pick up the girls early three days in a row. Now, when Liam implied that he sees more of Kate and Amy than I do, he wasn't wrong. And even if he didn't mean to knock me down by pointing this out, it still hurt. He doesn't know how acutely I feel that loss.

And I suspect that Liam is avoiding me during drop-off and pickup this week. Although, to be fair, when I pick up the girls on Tuesday he's busy talking to Blade's mother.

"The green playdough disappeared today," he's telling her. "It's not clear where it went, although I have a theory. Anyway, we make the playdough ourselves from organic flour. So if Blade has green poops, you don't need to panic."

"Good to know," Blade's mother is saying as Kate and Amy and I leave.

The girls and I visit the park on Tuesday evening. I push the stroller up that hill by myself, and then chase the girls around alone when it's time to saddle up and go home.

Sweating, I push the stroller home. I can't help but think of the time that Liam was at my side. He'd come to the park every night if I asked him to.

For a few weeks, my subconscious prods. *Then he's gone.*

Right. Nothing is easy. He must feel it, too. Or he'd be texting me to hook up later.

By the time my girls are asleep, Liam still hasn't returned the text I sent him earlier. When he finally does, it's late and he tells me he's working really hard on his thesis research.

But he doesn't come over the next night, either. Or the next. And by Friday I'm positive he's ghosting me. And there's a little voice inside me whispering how much it will hurt when our little fling is over, whether that happens now or at the end of summer.

I'm trying not to listen to that inner voice, because I'm not ready for it to end. After the girls go to sleep, I gather my courage and call him. "Hi, stranger," I say when he answers.

"Hi," he says softly. He doesn't say anything else. There's this awkward silence between us, and this uneasiness is new and scary.

"I miss you," I blurt. And boy, it's the truth. I miss the sex, but also the adult conversation. Liam is both smart and fun. I can't stay away. I can't stop thinking about him.

"I miss you, too," he says immediately.

There. That sharp awkwardness dissipates. I can breathe again.

He continues. "I know I haven't been around this week. But it's nothing you did wrong. I've just been too inside my own head to figure my shit out."

Inside his head. I know what that means. And I know it's partly because I turned down his offer to take the girls to the climbing wall. I get it. It was a cowardly move on my part, but I can't risk my girls falling for him and then he leaves.

I want to explain myself, but instead I hear myself say, "Come over. Drink some wine with me on the front porch and tell me your troubles. The doctor is in." I add that last bit with a smile. I hope he hears it.

"Will you wear a sexy doctor costume?" His joke lacks some of his usual energy, but he's trying.

"Don't push your luck."

He laughs, and then tells me he'll be right over.

Twenty minutes later, we're drinking wine on the porch as planned. There are two chairs, but we sit on the top step instead, because we're closer to each other that way. It's a lovely night. On this side of Michigan, the sky remains light until ten at night in midsummer. Birds are singing in the trees, and Liam's biceps are challenging both cuffs of his polo shirt. There's beautiful scenery everywhere I look.

I'm so happy right now I don't even recognize myself.

"You look very..." Liam smiles at me. "...Beautiful tonight."

"Beautiful wasn't the word you were going to use, was it?" I ask.

"Fine. My first thought was fuckable," he admits. "I haven't gotten you naked in days, and my inner horny teenager is starved for it. But you are also very beautiful."

"My inner teenager likes the attention," I admit. "Although you didn't have to wait all week, you know."

Liam winces. "Yeah. Sorry about that. I was trying to sort out my head without any input from my dick."

"And how did that go?"

He leans over and kisses my jaw. "My head likes you a whole lot, too." He straightens and puts a hand over his heart. "I've got it bad, Sadie. I'm more invested in you than you are in me."

I start to answer, but he gently cuts me off. "That's not your fault; it's just my cross to bear."

I take a big gulp of my wine and try to process that. "But you're the one who's leaving."

"I know," he says miserably.

"And even if you weren't, I can't afford to be so invested. It's more complicated for me."

"True." He sighs.

"I need to give my girls a stable home. But their dad couldn't make it to their second birthday without cheating. I can't have you in their lives when you and I are a temporary thing."

He looks like he wants to argue with me. *I'm already in their lives*. But Liam is a smart man. He resists the urge to tangle us up in another argument. He leans in and kisses me instead.

Liam is a freaking *genius*. Because the minute his generous lips press against mine, I forget all the tension between us. I set my wine glass down and wrap an arm around his neck. *Yes. More.*

He lets out a helpless little groan and kisses me more deeply. Two kisses become ten kisses. And then we're making out like horny teenagers on my front porch, while joggers pass by and dogs bark.

And then my phone rings, which is probably a blessing. I don't need to give my neighbors a show. Even so, it takes until the third ring until Liam and I can bear to pull away from each other.

"Wow," Liam says, panting. "Sorry."

"I'm not," I say, picking up the phone. The ringing already stopped. But it starts right up again. *Brynn calling*, it says.

She's only a couple weeks away from her due date, so I feel a frisson of excitement when I see her name. I answer immediately this time. "Hey! Any news?" I ask.

"Well..." She sounds hesitant. "I got a little situation here."

"What's that?"

"Tom is fishing with Braht."

"Fishing? That's something they do?"

"Yeah, because Tom hates golf. They don't catch any actual fish, but it's some kind of manly ritual. I don't get it. But anyway, Tom isn't answering his phone and I think I'm in labor."

"Okay, deep breaths. How are you feeling?"

"Well, at first it was just a back ache. But now it's like someone is *squeezing me in a motherfucking vice*, okay?"

"All right," I say calmly.

"Tom's not answering his phone!"

"Yes, but it's going to be okay." I'm using my Calm Doctor Voice. "They're only a few miles away, and it'll get dark soon. And labor takes a *long* time. Why don't you start timing your contractions? Do you need company?"

"No, I'm okay. I'll get the kitchen timer."

"I'm here if you need me."

"Thanks," she grunts.

"Is everything all right?" Liam asks when I hang up. "Is your friend going to have the baby?"

"It sure sounds like it. She's freaking out, although the baby probably won't show up until tomorrow."

"Do you need to go over there? I could stay here."

I just stare for a moment at the beautiful, kind man on my porch. I know I shouldn't compare Liam and Decker all the time, but the contrast is so striking. If Decker thought he was about to have sex and then instead I left to go help a friend? He'd lose his everloving mind.

"Sadie?"

I realize I never answered the question. "Sorry. Got a little distracted there for a second. Tom should be back with Brynn at any time. Now where were we?"

"Foreplay," he says with a smile, and my nipples tighten.

"Right. Let's go inside first, okay?"

"Good plan." He winks at me and gathers up the wine bottle and the glasses.

We relocate to my sofa. But two kisses later, the phone rings again. "I'm scared," Brynn says immediately. "Four minutes apart is close, right?"

Hmm. It is, but it's not an emergency. Or is it? "Well..."

"Can you please come over? A SMALL HUMAN IS TRYING TO CLAW ITS WAY OUT OF MY BODY!"

I have to hold the phone away from my ear to prevent deafness.

"Go," Liam mouths.

"I'll be right over," I tell Brynn.

———

Liam has promised to stay with the girls. They're fast asleep so there's no need for me to be concerned about the whole "Where is mommy and why is Liam-our-favorite-person-in-the-world here?" They'll sleep at least until 7 a.m. Plenty of time for me to visit Brynn and then return home without them realizing I ever left.

As I drive toward Brynn's place in Eastown, I feel like the relaxed, more experienced friend on her way to calm the newbie. I can hold her hand and remind her that if she goes to the hospital too early, they'll just send her home.

But Brynn is panting and pacing when I arrive. She's wearing only a sports bra and some yoga pants. It's a good plan. She's about to run a marathon. Figuratively speaking.

She's mid-contraction when I get there, so I just drop my purse and keys by the door and grab ahold of her. "I got you," I say. "Breathe. Breathe."

When it passes, she looks at me and says, "Motherfucker."

I nod. "How far apart are they?"

Silently she holds up the kitchen timer. The readout says two and a half minutes.

"Oh," I say carefully. But inside, my panic meter is climbing quickly toward the red zone. "All right." I'm using my Crazy

Person Voice, the one I need when one of my patients seems potentially unhinged. "Let's get you to the hospital," I say. "Nowish."

"'Kay," she pants with wide eyes.

"Where is your suitcase?" I do not want to deliver Brynn's baby on her kitchen floor. We eat in that kitchen. Often.

Brynn waddles toward the front closet when suddenly the door bursts open and there stands Ash. I swear to God, she appears like Wonder Woman, all fierce and glowing, highlighted by the last orange streaks of light in the sky behind her. It's all very dramatic. She's also carrying a roll of paper towels, a bunch of empty black trash bags, and a bucket of water.

"Ash?" Brynn asks. "What are you doing?"

"I am absolutely horrified by this entire prospect and I do not want to look at your stretching vagina while you birth a tiny human, but goddammit, I will do it. And I came prepared!"

All she needs is a blowtorch and a pair of goggles. I suddenly start laughing. And Brynn starts laughing, and then her laugh turns into a groan, and then all three of us are groaning through it together. When she's done, I tell Ash to get Brynn to the car. "I'll grab her bag," I say. "Ash, leave the uh, supplies. You're sitting with Brynn in the back seat."

"I think it's safer if I grab her bag and drive," Ash says, panic lacing every syllable.

"I don't care who's holding me," Brynn pants. "But get me to the hospital. And call Tom again!"

———

Ash is driving like the wind. When I say driving like the wind, I mean driving like the wind in a dead calm. She's going twelve miles an hour.

"A little hustle," I suggest. Kindly. Yet with intensity. Then I give up. "Ash, come on! We are not having this baby in the car!"

"I don't want to jostle her inner...stuff," Ash says. The car holds steady at twelve.

Suddenly I scream, "Placenta!" It's a fake out. There's no placenta here in the back of the Toyota. But it works. Ash's eyes grow ten sizes in the rearview mirror. Then she floors it. It's a smooth 35 all the way to the hospital.

Just as we get her up to the front doors, Tom and Braht pull up. The car has barely stopped moving when Tom leaps out, wearing an adorable fishing hat. He's sunkissed and worried as he rushes to Brynn. "Baby, I'm so sorry. I thought we had two weeks! I never would've gone fishing if I thought for even a second that..."

"Shush," she says, grabbing hold of his hands. Ash and I sweep open the double doors to the hospital and usher them through. "Baby wants out early. Who knew? When this is over you can bring me a really great sandwich and we'll call it good."

"Okay," he agrees. "Anything."

"A Cuban panini," she threatens.

"I'll import it from Cuba if you want," Tom blabbers. It's clear that the coaching I offered Tom has gone well.

We all take the elevator up to the third floor, where the labor and delivery department is. The staff ushers the happy couple right past the nursing station while Braht, Ash, and I just stand there, outside the doors, watching them go.

Ash reaches for Braht and says, "I don't want to ever go through that."

He squeezes her hand. "I totally agree."

I just sigh, and tears well up in my eyes. "Guys," I whisper. "Brynn is having a baby. Our Brynn. A baby!"

"I'm glad I brought this," Braht says and pulls out a flask from his summer blazer that I notice is printed with tiny lobsters all over it. Apparently, he dressed up for fishing. Then I realize that Tom was fishing, and Braht was probably just there for emotional support.

"Let's do this!" I say, "the waiting room is over there."

———

I was right about one thing. Births take a long time.

Hours pass. After a little tibble of the flask, we all switch to bad hospital coffee. Ash and Braht cuddle on one of the couches while looking at real estate listings on Braht's tablet. Then she pushes him away because he's annoying her. Then he does a little song and dance, literally, and slinks up beside her. They're too cute.

Watching them together makes me want to talk to Liam. But is that really fair? I can't expect him to be half a couple when I'm feeling clingy, and then push him away an hour later.

The problem is that I do want to be half a couple. I'll always want that. But it doesn't matter what I want, when Liam is unavailable. He says he's invested, but he's leaving in the fall.

Also, he's too young for me. I've been traded in for a younger model once already, and it broke apart my family. I won't let that happen again.

It doesn't mean I don't wish things were different. If Liam was five years older and finished with his Ph.D., it might all turn out differently.

If if if...

My phone chimes, and I feel my heart flutter. Maybe all my heavy thoughts zoomed through the West Michigan electromagnetic field and reached Liam, because he's texting me.

Or, possibly, he's been on my sofa for too long alone and he's just bored.

How are you? he asks.

I'm at the hospital, and as far as we know in the waiting room, things are good. The baby could be here any minute.

That's great, he says. ***But how are YOU?***

It makes me smile that he asks.

I'm good. Anxious. Nervous. Happy for her, but good. And you?

Girls are fast asleep. I'm binging on Netflix. I've missed you this week and I really want

I only see half of the text because Tom comes through the door, wearing his little daddy scrubs. He looks exhausted and his hair is sticking out in a hundred different directions, as if someone were mauling him.

And maybe someone was. "We have a son!" he yells.

And then we just all lose it. I mean, come on. Brynn and Tom...they have a *baby*. A *family!*

The three of us just rush him, sobbing. Braht's tears aren't so surprising, but Ash is the wild card here. The mascara is running down her face and she's crying like she's just watched *Beaches* for the first time. We all hug him. It's really ridiculous, this swelling of emotion. There should be a soundtrack. Then the proud daddy shows us a picture.

Braht takes his phone and studies it. "He looks just like you! Combover and all!"

"What?" Tom cries and grabs the phone. "That's a shadow, asswipe." Tom flips to a different picture and then smooths his hair down. There's no combover. It's just stressed-out-about-to-be-a-daddy hair. And hands Braht back the phone.

That baby? Little scrunchy red face, angry at his ordeal that he's just been through—he's just plain perfect.

"I want to hold him," I demand.

"You're in line behind me!" Ash yelps.

15 THE GLORY OF A WICKED TONGUE

Liam

AFTER TOO MANY days of hardly talking to Sadie, without seeing her, without being around her or under her or inside her...I had sort of hoped tonight would end a little differently. I'm so hungry for her. It's the kind of hunger that craves only one thing. Say, when you want nachos and nothing else will do. Not hummus and carrots. Not chips and dip. Nope. You want the nachos.

I want Sadie's nachos. Bad.

The girls stay asleep the whole time she's gone. I check on them to ensure they're breathing. Amy is curled around Piggypoo, one stubby leg sticking out of the blanket. Kate's eyes are screwed shut, as if sleeping requires great concentration.

I'm pretty attached to these little girls. I don't really let myself think about that too much. Sadie is right that they need stability. And I'm the jerk who's leaving for Europe in a couple of months.

I'm a little tired of Netflix, so I wander around and straighten up Sadie's house a bit. You can learn a lot about a person by being in their space. Sadie is full bookshelves and intellect and warmth.

She's soft fabrics and soothing colors and scents. She's wine and marcona almonds.

And she's a plate of fucking nachos. I want her so bad.

I don't have nachos. Instead, I have more *Game of Thrones* on TV. I watch several episodes in Sadie's bedroom, and all the sexy parts remind me of Sadie. Okay, not really because Sadie would never wear a dress with no butt and a leather corset. But fourteen-year-old Liam is horny and everything with two tits makes him think of Sadie.

It grows later and later, and I begin to fight sleep. I'm comfortable on Sadie's bed, and it smells like her. Four battles, three dragons, and two on-screen orgies later, I fall asleep thinking pleasant thoughts about her.

I am curled blissfully inside the cool blackness of unconsciousness when someone warm and soft snuggles close to me in the bed.

Sadie. It's wonderful to feel her presence, but I'm too asleep to move.

Smooth hands begin to stroke my sleepy limbs. Soft lips kiss my neck. It's pure bliss to be loved on while drowsing. I'm hovering in a delicious uncertainty between sleep and sex. It could really go either way.

But then Sadie moans.

Wake up! fourteen-year-old Liam screams. *What if she wants to touch our dick!*

He makes a great point.

"*Sadie*," I croak, pulling her into my arms. "I missed you."

"Missed you so much," she breathes against my chest. "All week," she adds as her mouth drifts wickedly down my belly.

I may be sleepy, but I'm not a stupid man. I yank down my boxers, kicking them under the sheets. And three pulse-pounding seconds later, Sadie's lips reach my cockhead.

"Yeah, honey," I encourage her. "Kiss me."

With a moan, she opens her mouth and bathes me with her

wicked tongue.

"Take more," I say, gathering her hair into my hand.

She sits up only long enough to toss her sundress over her head. Then she leans right back down and deepthroats me, one hand at the base of the cock, the other reaching up to touch my torso. It's so good that I moan too loudly for a house with toddlers.

Then Sadie gives a good hard suck, and fourteen-year-old Liam faints dead away.

But twenty-nine-year-old Liam wants more than just a world-class BJ. "Come here," I croak. "I need to hold you." I hook my arms under Sadie's and tug her upward.

She scrambles up my body until she's lying right on top of me, panting, staring down at me with a wild look in her eyes.

The wave of tenderness for her that washes over me is so strong it's startling. I push the waves of soft hair off her face and smile. "Are you okay?"

"Absolutely."

"Is there a new baby?"

"Yes! A *boy*." Her eyes tear up. "They named him Zachary Michael Spanner."

"Aw," I say. "Zach Spanner. He sounds like a superhero."

Sadie's voice is rounded with awe. "Brynn did it! He's so small and fragile and *alive*. I already love him so much!" Her gaze turns hungry, and she dives into a kiss, and I kiss her back with enough energy to power the sun. *Yes, yes, yes!* I don't even know which Liam is chanting that. We're of the same mind on the subject of Sadie.

We both reach for her underwear and Sadie yanks them down and kicks them away. She's straddling me now, and then, with a slow but easy slide down that takes my breath away, she welcomes me home, inch by delicious inch. I shudder gratefully as I sink into her wet heat. "*Oh, baby,*" I whisper against her lips. "Fuck me, honey."

"Say it again." She grinds her hips against me, pushing me inside her so far I fill her up.

"Fuck..." I lift my hips suddenly and deepen our connection. "...Me."

"Yes," she pants, and she starts to ride me. It's slow at first, but then she's riding me with a passion and speed that seems uncontained. God. This woman. "Yes!" she cries. Or maybe I cry it, because YES.

Now I'm bucking like a rodeo star. A heat grows between us, our skin slaps. Each thrust and buck sends a shiver of bliss through me and Sadie seems to shiver at the same time. Together we sprint toward the finish line. It's fast and frantic and just what I needed. I jack my hips off the bed over and over. "Can't wait any longer," I gasp, as a warmth in my balls warns me that this perfect moment is almost over. "You're making me come."

"Oh!" It's a high-pitched cry. "Liam," she sobs, shuddering over me.

I strain upwards one more time and clasp our two bodies tightly together. I can't tell where she stops and I begin.

Then we collapse together in a sweaty heap of joy and exhaustion.

———

Unfortunately, sweaty heaps of joy and exhaustion are not good at getting up and going home. About seven seconds after my orgasm I fall back into blissful slumber in Sadie's bed.

The next thing I register is a bug crawling up my arm. Only this is a very chatty bug, and it's singing the "Itsy Bitsy Spider" song.

My eyes fly open, and when they do, I find that I'm staring right into Amy's sweet hazel eyes. "Wiam," she says around her pacifier. "Up now."

And I would get up. Except I'm buck naked and underneath her mother. We're still wrapped up in each other.

I panic. Thankfully, panic is the mother of improvisation. Or something. "Did you really wake me up from my sleepover without bringing Piggypoo, too?" I ask. "Where's Piggypoo?"

Amy turns on her heel and trots out of the room to retrieve him.

I waste no time rolling Sadie off me, sliding out of bed and grabbing my khaki shorts off the floor. My underwear is God knows where, but this is an emergency. I'm just zipping up when Amy walks back into the room, her pig crammed under her arm.

"That's better," I say. "Now let's see about that saggy diaper you're wearing."

On the bed, Sadie's eyes pop open in alarm. *Shit!* she mouths.

I lean over and scoop Amy off the floor, leaving Sadie alone in the bed. I'll give Sadie a moment to get over her surprise, but the truth is that this is not a disaster. Kate and Amy are very young, and years away from understanding what sex is. They don't really have an opinion on my sleeping over.

Carrying Amy into the girls' room, I put her on the floor next to the changing table. "Drop 'em," I say, tugging down her pj pants.

Four seconds later she's fresh and clean, and her sister is blinking at me from the other crib. Kate gives me a big, happy smile.

"You, too, right?" I beckon, and she stands up. When I lift her up to my body, she's warm and sleepy. She wraps her chubby little arms around my neck, and I give her a squeeze. Who could resist?

After a second diaper exchange, I pick up one toddler on each arm and carry them out into the hall. I hear the shower going in the master bath. "Let's go downstairs and see what you've got in your kitchen. Do you know how to make pancakes?"

"No," Kate says at the exact moment that Amy says, "yes."

"Excellent," I say.

16 SMALL PANIC ATTACK. BIG PANCAKES.

Sadie

I MESSED UP. **Big time.**

These are my thoughts as I rush into the bathroom for the world's fastest shower. The hot spray of water judges me as I hastily wash Liam off my thighs.

A better mother wouldn't let this happen. I shouldn't have a younger lover. If I didn't, he wouldn't be so deliciously appealing. I couldn't lose my mind, wake him up out of a sound sleep to ride him like a pony. And then collapse beside him in peaceful, sated slumber.

Seriously, how did I let that happen?

You know how, my hormones scold me. *Because he's the hottest thing you've ever tasted.*

Oh yeah. That.

After showering I get dressed at top speed. Poor Liam is currently shouldering all my parental responsibilities. Throwing on yesterday's sundress, I pause for a moment to pop a birth control pill, because that's one thing I won't goof up.

Then I hurry downstairs.

The sight in the kitchen gives me heart palpitations. But not because there's flour dusting much of the countertop. Rather, it's the hot, shirtless guy holding my toddler and making a dump truck sound as Amy tips the measuring spoon over a bowl.

"Yes! Well done, little miss," he says, relieving her of the spoon. "Batter up!" he says, easing her to the floor and catching Kate, who's trying to climb him like a tree.

Aren't we all.

Liam easily rests Kate on one of his perfect arms, measures a half teaspoon of baking powder one-handed and then hands the spoon to Kate. "Beep beep beep," he says, making the sound of a truck backing up. "Look out below!"

Kate dumps the spoonful into the bowl and giggles.

"Awesome. Who wants to add the milk?"

"My do it!" Amy yells.

Boy, I need another minute of alone time to compose myself. Because I love this picture a little too much. I love Liam's ease with my girls. I love how calm he is at the center of toddler-induced mayhem.

It causes a little pain in my heart as I allow myself one more comparison to my former life. The truth is I never once saw Decker elbows-deep in kitchen chaos with a kid on one arm. Starting breakfast with twins in tow? He was more likely to captain a NASA expedition to Mars than he was to do this simple Saturday morning thing.

I feel like crying for no reason at all. Clearly I'm on some kind of emotional overload. Maybe coffee will help.

Sliding into the kitchen, I go right for the coffee grounds.

"Mama!" Amy says. "Wiam making pancakes."

"That is amazing," I say in a wobbly voice. "What a lucky girl you are."

"Sorry about the *mess*," he says, casting a glance in my direction. And I know he doesn't just mean the flour on the counter, but the bigger mess of waking up naked in my bed.

"You know," I say with a small sigh. "Messes shouldn't scare me so much. It's going to be fine."

Liam's smile is so filled with relief, that I now feel like an ogre. This man wants to make pancakes with us on Saturday morning, and I said no to that before? I'm clearly insane.

"Which frying pan should I use?" he asks, casting an eye on the cookware hanging from the rack over the sink.

"Oh, no. You want this." I pull a double-burner griddle out of a lower cabinet.

"Ooh," he says. "Mommy has the fancy pancake griddle."

Kate giggles. She's gazing at Liam as if he invented fun.

And in my life, I guess he did.

Here's the tricky thing about being a shrink—sometimes you notice that you're doing something that's exactly contrary to the advice you'd give your patients.

I'm having one of those moments right now.

If I had a single mom in my office telling me there was a lovely guy in her life who was kind to her kids—and yet she was giving him the stiff arm? I'd tell her: "Be kind to yourself. Don't push away the good people in your life, especially if you think you don't deserve them. Let people surprise you."

I'm such a hypocrite.

Also, I need caffeine.

Ten minutes later I'm sipping from a mug of coffee, but Liam's is cooling on the countertop. The man has his hands full right now as he puts pancakes on the griddle with "help" from my daughters.

"How about a few of these?" he asks, holding up a bag of chocolate chips. Meanwhile, Kate waves the spatula around like a ninja. "A guy needs to make smiley faces in his pancakes sometimes."

Good. Lord. It's a miracle I'm not just a puddle of my former self right now. This is some serious mommy porn I'm watching. *Shirtless guy feeds toddlers before eight a.m.* I walk over to the high cabinet where I keep the ramekins. "We could make smiley faces with dried organic currants," I say, just to be a pain in the ass.

Liam makes a face of disgust as I take the chocolate chips from his hand and pour some into a ramekin. "Joking! Here."

He gives me a big, hot smile. Okay, it probably wasn't meant to be hot, but I feel flutters down below.

"Choc-it!" Kate yells, grabbing for the ramekin.

"Easy," Liam says with a laugh. "That's for my artwork. Come here and I'll show you."

I set the table and pour the sippy cups of milk. And Liam manages to serve up two smiley pancakes—one for each girl—at exactly the same moment, in exactly the same size. This is a man who knows his way around toddlers.

"Not cut it!" Amy yells when I approach her plate with a knife. She picks up the pancake in two hands and takes a bite right out of the side of its face.

"Okay, right." I back away. Forks are optional today, then. No big deal.

Liam takes advantage of this moment of quiet to quickly pour six more pancakes onto the griddle. He leans over his work, dotting them with chocolate chips.

I step closer to him and put a hand on his lower back. "Thank you," I whisper.

"For trashing your kitchen?"

"No." He glances at me and I give him a shy smile. "For being so amazing all the time."

His eyes get very warm, and I just want to stay right here in that blue-eyed gaze as long as I can. "This might be a good time to confess that I didn't make smiley faces on my own pancakes."

"No?" I look down at the griddle. Side by side, two of them have a different design—little bullseyes in their centers. "Those are...?"

"Boobs," he whispers. "My inner fourteen-year-old has a dirty mind. He can't shut it off sometimes."

"Drink your coffee," I whisper, handing him the mug. "Sit down. Let me finish these for you. Or go put on a shirt because *my* inner fourteen-year-old has her tongue hanging out all the time, too."

He gives me a wicked, wicked smile and then runs upstairs to find his shirt.

I only have a few moments to panic and draft the speech I ought to be giving the girls. "He's only visiting," or "Liam is Mommy's special friend," or "Liam isn't permanent. Can you spell per-ma-nent?"

But I don't give any of those speeches. Liam is back, shirt on, and looking like a nerdy Adonis. What a combination. In fact, he's so fast that I don't even have time to process anything.

I have the pancakes stacked neatly on a plate. I'm about to serve his to him, when he reaches over, grabs one, blows on it a little, and takes a big bite. "Needs a little butter," he says, then reaches to the other side of me, grabs the butter knife and spreads a little pat on what's left of his pancake.

And I can't breathe. Liam is standing here, fully clothed, in my kitchen, eating pancakes straight from the griddle, and it's the sexiest thing I've ever seen.

I wish I was that pancake.

He winks at me. Winks! The flirt.

"I gotta eat and run," he says, grabbing another pancake for the road.

He grabs his backpack, gives the girls fist bumps, and kisses me on the cheek, chastely, and then starts to head out the back door.

"Hey!" I call, and he turns around, a cocky little grin on his face. And a bit of scruff from not shaving yet. Oh, how I like that scruff. "Thanks," I say. "For last night," I add.

"Totally my pleasure," he says with a glint in his eye.

"Not that," I whisper. "Staying here so I could help with, you know, the baby?"

"I know. What else could I possibly mean?"

What else, really. He walks a couple steps closer to me and checks to see if the girls are watching. They're not. Then he leans in and whispers, "Let's just say you owe me one."

I gulp. I literally gulp. I'm happy to owe him one. Or two. Or however many he wants.

"Okay," I say. And if you can say okay all husky like, I do, because *oooookaaaaaay*.

This time he actually leaves.

I turn around to find the girls and take a deep breath gearing up to explain the complexities of my relationship with Liam and why he was here and why he made them pancakes, but before I can say anything, Kate head-butts Amy and then Amy, in a fit of fury, turns Piggypoo into a ninja and full-on attacks Kate. Man, that Piggypoo has a mean kick. Inwardly, I'm all *Good for you!*, but outwardly, I have to handle this.

So maybe the conversation with the girls will have to wait.

Or maybe it doesn't have to happen at all.

Huh.

17 MEG. THE BALLBUSTER.

Liam

A WEEK LATER, it's like Sadie and I never had a tiff. And it's sort of like we're dating. For real. After the accidental sleepover and how completely underwhelmed her girls were, she told me tentatively, "Well. Maybe we don't have to be a complete secret. But there still has to be firm boundaries."

"Okay," I said. "I won't ask them to call me Dad. They can call me PawPaw."

She laughed but also gave me a nudge. I guess PawPaw is out.

Sadie and I just dropped the girls off at their dad's. I sat in the car, but I could still feel that dick nozzle's bad energy wafting through the air like a fart. I still haven't met him, but I admit to being totally curious.

What kind of superhuman won over Sadie? He must have a seriously impressive resume, a genius IQ, and a giant dick.

Wait—he can't have a genius IQ. Because he left her. He must be as dumb as a bag of hammers. And I really don't want to think about her ex's dick. At all.

I'd rather think about my own, because Sadie and I are about to have another weekend together. This is wildly exciting, and I'm already sporting a semi. My plans are: sex, sleeping in, late night pizza in bed, and more sex. It's going to be epic. And since the girls are away, I can hold Sadie all night and then start everything over again in the morning.

We'll be spending the night at my house for the first time, and I can hardly wait. Just as soon as she packs a bag.

Oh, the things I hope she puts in that bag.

I've already panic-cleaned my place and shopped for supplies. Like whipped cream and strawberries. Make of that what you will. Both Liams—the fourteen-year-old and the grown-up—have big plans.

But then... Hold up. "There's a car in your driveway."

"What the..." She inhales.

It's an old red Volvo and it's crammed full of stuff. There's no way the driver could see anything in the rearview mirror on account of the boxes and suitcases. I also see a big plant, and what looks like camping gear.

I put the car in park and Sadie is off like it's the start of the hurdles event at a track meet. "Sadie?" I call.

"It's my sister!" she calls as she's running. I can't tell if her voice is excited or panicked.

But I know how I feel—depressed. If Sadie's sister is here, for whatever reason, our weekend at my house just went up in a whoosh of flame.

Goodbye to naked pizza in bed.

I take a moment of silence behind the wheel of my car, just to tamp down my disappointment. Just as I'm about to climb out, though, Sadie's sister opens a door and plops into the back seat, followed quickly by Sadie, who buckles up in the front.

Meg leans forward. She pats my shoulder. "Hi, Liam. You look gorgeous as ever. I absolutely approve of the fact that you're boinking my sister. She needs it bad. I, on the other hand, need a martini."

I can shift gears just as quickly as the next guy. With a glance at Sadie, I say, "Rose's?"

"Rose's," she confirms.

———

I drive over to the restaurant on Reed's Lake where, if you're lucky, you can get a seat out on the deck right by the water.

We are not lucky. We're inside, on the covered patio, and it's fine. They've opened the floor-to-ceiling windows so the ceiling fans can stir the humid air.

Above us, there's a giant anchor made from rope, serving as a rustic chandelier. I keep staring at it, wondering who makes things like that. Who woke up one morning and decided the world needed a giant anchor made from rope?

We've ordered our drinks and an appetizer and Meg starts talking about some doctor she was dating in Atlanta. Blah blah blah. He lied to her in a pretty spectacular way, which stinks. But I can tell we'll be here all night hearing about it.

I watch her lips move, but tune her out. There are words. Lots of them. One after another. Meg hasn't changed a bit. She always was a talker.

We went to the same high school. But I don't think of her as a classmate. To me, she was Sadie's Sister. I'm pretty sure that every time I bumped into Meg I always asked the same things. *How's Sadie? Is she still in school? Is she travelling? Is she coming back?*

To which Meg would reply: *Obsess much, Liam?* Or maybe *Fuck off. Grow a pair and ask her yourself.* Meg was a bit of a firecracker then. Now she's matured into more of a fireball. Or maybe a ballbuster.

Or a cockblocker.

She and Sadie aren't much alike. Everything Meg does shouts *notice me!* For example, she's wearing a tight cowboy shirt and pigtails, Daisy Dukes, and strappy heels in bright red. I mean, she looks great, but if I was driving eight hundred miles, I'd dress for comfort.

Sadie, on the other hand, isn't wearing flashy colors or fuck-me heels. But damn if she doesn't turn me on more. I reach under the table and place my hand on Sadie's thigh, luxuriating in the thin silkiness of her skirt.

I'm trying not to harbor a grudge at Meg for interrupting all the wicked plans I had for this weekend. But it's not working. I'm totally harboring here. I'm Pearl fucking Harbor. Not even a plate of root chips with goat cheese dipping sauce in front of me can put a damper on it.

So I just try to focus on Sadie. I squeeze her thigh, imagining I'm rubbing my body up against her.

Suddenly, she leans in close to my ear and whispers, "If you rub me anymore, I'm going to explode."

Busted. I lean back, putting a more respectable distance between us. But not by choice.

I turn my focus to the dip and the beer in my glass. And to Meg, who is clearly in turmoil. I will focus on her and not on Sadie and her luscious curves that are lurking underneath the swaths of fabric.

We're totally peeling that off her later, fourteen-year-old Liam says.

I hope to God he's right.

Sadie

When we pulled into my driveway and I saw Meg's car, I just knew that my sister's latest drama was about to suck me in. And that any plans I had of, well, the *fun* kind of sucking just evaporated.

Now my sister is on her second martini. I'm trying to listen but also to size her up. Meg was always the dramatic one, and today is no different. She's dressed to seduce. The mother in me wants to cover her up.

We've been here a half hour already and she hasn't asked a single question about me, or inquired as to what plans of ours she's interrupting. With Meg, everything is always about her. She's the little sibling. I guess they get away with that sort of thing.

Liam's hand is a welcome presence on my thigh, which makes it all easier to take.

"I'm *heartbroken*," Meg whines, taking a big gulp of her martini. She's playing the part of Heartbroken Lover to the max. "If I'd known he was married, I never would have slept with him."

After all that I've been through, I can't believe my sister was sleeping with a married man. "Didn't you get suspicious when he said his house was being fumigated six weeks in a row?"

"Termites are really bad in the South, okay?" Meg whines.

I know nothing of termites, so I guess I don't have an opinion about that. On the other hand, this guy sounds like a loser straight from loserville. "Is he even a doctor? Was that part true?"

"He's a podiatrist," she sniffles.

"Oh," I say, doing my best not to make even one more negative comment.

"In training," Meg adds.

Liam shoves another chip in his mouth. I think he's trying not to speak up, too.

"I went ahead and fell in love with him," Meg says with a sigh. She takes another big gulp of the martini and it's gone.

"But he was married," I say and my voice is a little weak. "He's not available."

"Not true!" she yelps. "He told me he was single. And then later when I found out, he told me he wanted to leave his wife for me. What an asshole. I want no part in that." She waves to the waiter for another drink.

I may need one soon too.

"I just wanted to have a little strings-free sex. You know? No commitment. No expectations. Just like you and Liam! And then I had to get feelings for the big oaf. And then he had feelings for me and..."

Liam turns white and looks the other way.

Oh Meg, shut up! I should be giving Liam a blowjob right now. Instead I've subjected him to my sister. This is bad. I need to change the topic. "So why did you leave? Why all the stuff? In your car? I mean, that's more than a visit, Megs."

"Because I'm over it."

"What?"

"All of it. Antonio the foot doctor. His midlife crisis. Atlanta traffic. Casting directors with bad teeth." She sighs. "I just want to be carefree. I'm in my twenties!"

"For about three more weeks," I point out, because I'm evil.

She ignores me. "I should be having fun, not putting money down for a mortgage. And I'm over Atlanta. I've been there what? Two years? Trying the whole actress thing? It's no better than LA or New York. It's all just playing games. I need a fresh start."

Liam squeezes my leg. I don't even need to look at him to know what he's thinking. Meg is pushing thirty, but she acts like a college girl. And Grand Rapids is not going to hold her interest for long. Grand Rapids is just the place you return to to settle in and get a mortgage. It's not a place to sow your wild oats.

Like I'm doing with Liam.

I wonder if he can hear me gulp.

Just as I'm wondering what to say to my sister, I see Barb and Brad Thornapple walking toward us. They're friends of my parents. Well, not friends, exactly. More like they lived next to us when we were growing up. Meg and I moved out, our parents got a condo, and we all moved on.

But Barb still wants to get up in everyone's business. Her unwillingness to change is sort of comforting, really. And in spite of myself, I do like her. When Mom was really sick, Barb helped us all through it. She brought us casseroles and drove us to school, and somehow, despite her brashness, she wiggled into my heart. There is something refreshing about a person who will just say anything at all.

Barb is big and bold and bright, and she's spotted us. It's fair to say she's bearing down on us. Tonight she's wearing pink, orange, and yellow with beige pants. She looks like a walking scoop of sherbet. She's twice the size of Brad. When he stands behind her, which is frequently, he actually disappears. "Meg..." I whisper, trying to warn her about what's coming. About *who's* coming. The Walking Volcano.

"Don't get me wrong. The sex with Antonio was amazing," Meg continues, unfazed. "He would do this thing with his thumb and forefinger, sort of like this little swirly and hook thing..." She starts to demonstrate with her hands and I'm both horrified and interested. Barb interrupts before she can get too far.

"Meg! Sadie!" And Barb Thornapple is booming right at us. "It is so good to see you two. All grown up now!"

And with boobies, I want to say, but keep the snark on the inside.

"Brad and I just got back from Iceland! Can you believe it? We went to one of those outdoor hot tubs."

"Springs," Brad mumbles.

"Springs. And we went...in the *buff*," she shares with us, whispering that last part. I think Liam shivers. "Anywho! What are you girls up to? How are your parents? And, Meg, *look* at you! You've grown into such a beautiful young woman. And this must be your strapping boyfriend! You two would have beautiful babies!"

Barb motions from Meg to Liam, and my stomach drops right to the floor. Liam is sitting next to *me*. His hand is under the table, inching ever so closely to between my thighs, but Barb assumes Liam is with Meg?

Goddammit. Do I really look that much older than he does?

"Wouldn't they have cute babies?" Barb asks Brad. Brad

doesn't answer. "Your mom was just telling me the other day how she needs more grandbabies. Boys preferably. I mean, Sadie, with you being divorced and all, it's just going to be you and your girls. No hope for more, is there?" I couldn't get a word in even if I wanted to. "Are there going to be wedding bells for you two soon?" she asks, again to Meg and Liam.

I want to argue, I do. But I can't. Words are stuck in my throat. Nothing will come out. I think I'm dying. I think it's a panic attack. So this is what one feels like. It feels like I'm turning inside out. Of course, Barb assumes Meg is with Liam. Why wouldn't Liam choose young and supple Meg over her dried apricot sister? Clearly, they belong together.

I want to die.

Worse, I want to go home, watch *The Bachelor*, and eat actual dairy, non-organic ice cream. Straight from the tub. I won't even use a spoon. I'll just dig my face right into the container like a dog.

"Actually," Liam tries to say, but Meg beats him to it.

"This is Liam McAllister," she says. Loudly. "Liam is fucking my sister. They go at it all the time. He can't keep his hands off her. She left her husband ages ago. Because he was a prick. I'm home now because I'm starting over. I was fucking a podiatrist in Atlanta, but I'm done with him. Basically, I'm back in town to find a big dick to sit on and spin for a while. Any big dicks in Iceland?"

"There was one," Brad offers. Barb actually elbows him.

"Any other questions?" Meg asks.

Barb's lips have disappeared. I think she's swallowed them. "No," she says, simply. "I think I've got it."

If Barb stayed even one more minute I think my panic spiral would sweep me under. But—thank the heavens above—I see her eyes lock on someone else across the room. "Ooh! It's Bert and Becki! I wonder if they're still pretending their daughter is away at camp when she's actually moved in with her girlfriend. Excuse me…"

She hustles off.

An exhausted silence settles over our table. None of us make eye contact. My only comfort is Liam's hand under the table. It's practicing a spiral and hook thing against my thigh.

———

On the way home from Rose's, Meg passes out in the back seat of Liam's car. One minute she's ranting about how all the good men on Earth are either married or gay, and then she literally breaks off mid-sentence to slump down on the back seat.

The silence is beautiful. Except that Liam and I don't fill it with carefree banter. He looks so tense behind the steering wheel that I worry he'll break it right off of his own car.

"I'm sorry our weekend plans to stay at your place were ruined," I say. "But I think Meg needs me to be around."

"We can have nachos some other time," he says through a clenched jaw.

"Nachos?"

"Just a figure of speech."

I haven't heard that one before, but I am too wise to say so right now. "Can you come over and watch a movie with me?"

"Sure," he says. "I'll stay the night. Your sister doesn't care. In fact, I believe she encouraged me to boink you."

"That wasn't even the most embarrassing part of this day."

"No, it was not." He sighs. "Look, I'm going to grab my toothbrush and the dinner I made you."

"You made me dinner?" I gasp.

"Of course." He pulls up in front of his house. "Sadie, I *love* cooking for you."

There's a beat of silence between us while I try to absorb that.

He loves cooking for me, because it's not just sex. "Thank you," I breathe. "That was really nice."

I'm in so much trouble.

"I'll be right back with an Instant Pot full of butter chicken."

He gets out of the car, leaving me with my sad thoughts and a sister who's begun to snore.

If she stays asleep, I'm eating her share of butter chicken.

Liam comes out of his house a minute later with a small gym bag over one shoulder and a pot in his hands. He has to set the pot down for a second to check his mail. As I watch, he flips through a couple of envelopes...and then freezes.

He tosses all the mail except one envelope back in the box, picks up the pot, and comes back to me. I jump out of the car and open the trunk for him, so he has somewhere to set the pot down.

"What's the envelope?" I ask, and he grimaces.

"It's from the Child Study International. I think they're letting me know where I'm going in October." He lifts blue eyes to mine, and they're worried.

"Open it," I whisper, after we blink at each other for a second.

Wearing a grim expression, he slits the envelope open with one finger and pulls the paper out. He unfolds it quickly and...

"Rome," he says in the same voice that Russian dissidents might use to say "Siberia."

"Oh, wow," I say quietly. I'm not sure what to think about that, or what I'm allowed to say. "What a dump, honey. All those marble antiquities. And the gelato and excellent coffee."

He looks over the edge of the paper and gives me a sad smile. "October fifth is when I leave."

"That's..." I do the math. "Only a few weeks away." Okay, it's eight. But still.

Liam swallows. We're standing here trapped in our own misery, but there's nothing to be done about it. I don't know what to say.

Luckily, Megan wakes up with a snort. "I smell butter chicken," she grumbles.

"That's for me," I say automatically. I've had all the disappointments today that I can take.

"There's plenty for everyone," he says. "Let's go."

18 A LOUD WHINNYING NOISE

Liam

THAT NIGHT SADIE and I don't have sex. It's not because her sister is one room away. It's because we're sad.

If only Sadie would admit it. I wish she'd beg me not to leave. I'd probably still have to, but maybe we could try a long-distance relationship. People do that. It's a thing. I wonder what she'd say to that? Maybe that's why she's so quiet. Right now she's probably thinking about my moving away and it's caused all this silence. "What are you thinking about?" I whisper as I smooth down her hair.

"Meg," she says immediately.

It's a good thing it's dark in here so she can't see me flinch. Maybe I'm the only one who is going to lose sleep over Rome.

"...She must have suspected that guy was married. How could she not know?"

"No idea," I mumble.

"Meg makes poor life choices, and then I pick up the pieces."

"Seems like it," I say just to be nice. "Although you told me she flew up here when you needed her to help you throw Decker out."

"Oh, Liam. You're right." She gives me a little poke in the ribs. "You're a better person than I am for remembering that."

Sadie has no trouble telling me I'm a good man. And yet she doesn't see a future for us. I just don't get it. Doesn't she want a good man in her life, in her girls' lives? Why can't it be me?

I fall asleep holding her, and trying to think of a scenario where we work out as a couple.

But I can't.

In the days that follow, two things quickly become apparent. One—I wasted a perfectly good night in Sadie's bed, feeling sad when I should have been giving her orgasms. And two, her sister Meg is around all the time. She's cock-blocking me.

It's fast becoming a desperate situation. I have seven weeks with Sadie left, but now Meg is here and taking up a lot of Sadie's time.

Meg is, however, another pair of hands. So sometimes Sadie and I escape for a late dinner or a cocktail somewhere after the girls are down for the night. It's great spending time with her, right up to the point where I kiss her goodbye in the car and go home alone. Hello, back to being a teenager.

I'm not the only one who feels this way, either. Last night when Sadie kissed me good night she actually climbed into my lap until her ass tapped the car horn in the middle of our makeout sesh. "God, we have got to get Meg her own place," she'd whispered. "I'm taking her to see an apartment tomorrow. I found it on craigslist."

"Good plan," I'd said, diving in for one more kiss.

Let's just do it in the car! shouts fourteen-year-old Liam.

But alas, grown-ups can't expose their butts to their neighbors on Willow Drive. And even if Meg wouldn't mind me following Sadie upstairs and banging her into next Tuesday, we're not doing that.

I'm not sure why, but we're not.

Which is why I'm kneeling on Sadie's rug the next morning,

giving pony rides to Kate and Amy while the two women run out the front door.

"Mommy will be back in less than an hour!" Sadie calls from the doorway.

"Giddyup," Kate says, having already forgotten her mom. She gives me a little kick in the flank to make sure I understand my role.

I make a loud whinnying noise as the front door shuts.

Sadie didn't even ask me to watch the girls, but I offered. That's how eager I am to get Meg her own place to stay. Very, very eager. Eager enough to whinny and wobble around the rug for a solid hour, and then pretend to eat oats out of Amy's hand.

I've just enjoyed my second imaginary carrot in the imaginary barnyard when I hear a car pull up outside. My knees are grateful. But Sadie doesn't walk in like I expect her to. Instead, someone raps three times on the door. And then it opens. "Sadie? Girls? Daddy is here."

"Daddy?" Amy says.

"Giddyup," Kate insists from my back. "Faster."

I execute an awkward maneuver whereby I stand up without letting Kate slide to the floor. So I'm red-faced and wearing her like a scarf when a strange man appears in the living room doorway. He's wearing a polo shirt and a pair of khaki pants with creases so sharp that he might cut himself on them. And prissy deck shoes and a gaudy gold watch.

This is Sadie's ex? *Really?* When I came face to face with Decker, I expected someone fascinating. In my mind, he'd have to be both seriously attractive and magnetic. Artistic, maybe. This guy is your standard issue golf club member. He's attractive, I suppose, if you like 'em bland and preppy.

It must be a subconscious reflex that causes me to flex my pecs and biceps. Either that or I'm having some kind of rare but harmless muscle spasm.

"Who are you?" he asks.

"I think that's my line," I say coolly, even though I have a pretty good inkling. Also, I tighten my biceps. I can't help it. I blame fourteen-year-old Liam. *Punch him in the nuts!* my inner teen suggests.

Good thing I don't listen to him.

"Daddy!" Amy squeaks as she scurries over to stand at his feet. She raises her arms overhead, waiting to be picked up.

He ignores her, because he's too busy frowning at me. "Look, I have a company picnic today. And we just read the schedule and saw there's a bouncy castle. So I'm taking the girls. If you could just get their stuff together."

Kate squeals and wiggles, forcing me to bend over and set her gently on the floor. Meanwhile, my head is going to blow right off, I'm pretty sure. Because you do *not* say the words "bouncy castle" to a pair of two-year-olds if you can't follow through.

And he can't. Because there's one huge problem. "I don't know you," I say as calmly as I can. "And furthermore, Sadie didn't say a word about a company picnic. She's out with her sister for a bit, but I can have her call you when she gets back."

His face curls in displeasure even before I stop speaking. "I'm their dad. It makes no difference whether you know me or not. And who are *you?* Answer the question."

"The babysitter," I say from between clenched teeth.

"Wiam," Amy tries.

"Pony," Kate adds with a solemn nod.

Decker looks at his watch. "The picnic starts in fifteen minutes. I can't be late."

"Be that as it may, it's my job to stay with the girls unless Sadie tells me otherwise. So why don't you step outside and call her." My tone is chilly. Like, twenty-below-zero chilly. "Just because you woke up today and remembered you had..." *two children.* I can't say that out loud because it might hurt Amy or Kate's feelings. "...*A picnic,*" I say instead, "doesn't mean you can just show up and expect me to hand them over."

"Bouncy castle?" Kate asks as Decker turns and stomps out the door. I notice that he never once greeted his girls or spoke directly to them at all.

What a tool. Seriously, what was Sadie even thinking? He must be very, very good in the sack because Sadie has a high libido. Almost as high as mine.

It's really the only explanation that makes sense.

"Who's turn is it?" I ask the girls, trying to snap out of it.

They both clamor for the next ride, and so I load 'em both up there. Sorry, knees. And about four minutes later I hear Decker's car start again, and he drives away.

Either Sadie didn't answer, or she did answer and she didn't give him the answer he was looking for.

"Daddy?" Amy says, and she's starting to slide off my back. I freeze and then flatten myself onto the rug so she doesn't hurt herself on the dismount. She runs to the door. "Daddy?"

Oh shit.

"Daddddddyyyy," she wails.

When I glance at Kate, her face wobbles, too. "Bouncing," she says with a sniff. "Want to go now."

"Girls," I say with false cheer, leaping to my feet. "We can make our own Bungee Bouncing Palace. This is going to be great!"

Now I know why divorced parents sometimes spoil their children. Because Amy wailing "Daddy" out the front door is breaking my heart into teeny tiny shreds.

"Come on!" I gather her up and brush away her tears. "I have an idea."

Sadie

When I get home, the living room is empty. But there are giggles coming from upstairs.

"Okay. Backflip," Liam says. "You got this. On three."

I jog up the stairs, and I'm startled to hear that the noise is coming from my bedroom.

When I walk in, I'm still confused. And a little terrified. There's a...contraption strung up between the closet door and the door to the bathroom. Liam has tied several blue bungee cords—vaguely familiar, I think they're from a hook in my garage—to a harness made from... I squint. Yup, that's really two of my nursing bras tied together.

What the actual heck?

As I stare, Amy bounces on the bed. In the first place, that's strictly against the rules. If I let the girls bounce on my bed we'd have to get stitches at the E.R. at least once a week. She's holding Liam's hands, and the bungees give her extra lift. So she probably imagines herself to be super woman right now.

"Three...two...one..." Liam counts down and then grabs Amy by the diaper and flips her neatly around until she's executed a perfect layout backflip, and her stubby feet land back on the bed.

She lets out a shriek of glee that's nearly as high as a dog whistle. And then her sister follows up with: "Me me me my turn mine!"

"*Excuse* me," I say. It comes out sounding a little bitchy. But this little game isn't okay with me. "Are those really my bras? And the springs on the bed may never be the same."

Liam whips around to see me standing there. But the look on his face isn't the sheepish one I expect. It's red and hurt and angry and fit to burst with a few other emotions I can't even unpack on the fly. "They each get two more turns," he says in a clipped tone.

"But..."

Kate is already climbing into the harness.

"Did you get any calls while you were out?" Liam grunts, helping her.

"Yes, but..." *Decker.* That's who'd called me. I'd ignored the calls because ignoring Decker's calls gives me a thrill.

But why does Liam know that?

Uh-oh.

I step out of the room and pull out my phone. Sure enough, Decker called more than once. And when I listen to the message, my heart sinks. "Sadie, this is bullshit. Some dumbass kid won't hand over the girls and pack a diaper bag. There's a company picnic and a bouncy castle and Honey thought it would be fun if we brought the girls. Fix this. It starts in fifteen minutes." *Click.*

And all becomes clear. Liam's impromptu game and the look on his face are the direct result of Decker's latest moment in tone-deaf parenting.

Some dumbass kid. No, Liam is the smarter man. He did the hard thing, which was to tell two girls they couldn't have their dad and whatever pleasures the picnic held, because grown-ups have to say no sometimes even when it hurts.

I walk back into the bedroom just as Kate is collapsing in a red-faced, smiling heap on the bed after her final turn. "Bouncing," she sighs. "I wuv it."

"Almost as good as climbing," Liam agrees, giving her toe a playful tug.

"Time for a snack!" I say cheerfully. "Aunt Meg is going to give it to you."

They both go charging out of the room.

"Careful on the stairs!" I say, because I can't help it and that's what mothers do. Two seconds later I can hear the sound of two toddlers descending one stair at a time, on their little butts.

"Sadie..." Liam says.

I hold up a hand. "I clued in. Sorry. There's a voicemail and I get it now."

"He was *such* an asshole," Liam growls, his hands in fists.

"How can I make it up to you?" I want to soothe him. I want to unclench his fists and smooth those angry lines from his face.

"We're going on an errand," he says, tugging my hand and

leading me toward the stairs. "Meg!" he barks. "Gonna head out for a minute to the hardware store. Sadie needs a tool."

"Okay!" she calls from the kitchen. "I'll cut up some watermelon for the screaming mimis." That's her name for my girls.

Liam practically frog-marches me down the walk. We both get into his car and he practically peels away from the curb. I'm in a bit of a fog so I don't even notice when he makes just two turns and then pulls up in front of his house, where I've rarely been. "Let's go," he grunts.

I get out of the car and follow him up the short walk. But we're not at the hardware store. I'd assumed maybe something broke during the bungee bouncing. "Thought we needed a tool?"

"Oh, you definitely do," he says, "I have just the tool for you. And here I thought you'd already read Freud." He unlocks the door in a big hurry and pulls me inside. Then he pushes me up against the door and kisses me. It's a hot, angry *brand* of a kiss. Like he's so full of pent-up needs and fears that it needs to escape his soul. Via his tongue.

I gasp, my head hitting the door with a thunk. He tilts his head and kisses me again, his hard body caging me in, his hands skimming down my breasts.

And I give it right back to him, clutching his beautiful, angry face in both hands and slipping my tongue into his mouth.

He makes a startled noise and then grips me even more tightly.

And, *duh*. Now I get it. The tool Liam wants to give me is his own. And as his erection presses against my belly, I'm suddenly a hundred percent down with this plan. "Bedroom," I moan.

"Too far," he grunts. "Lift up your skirt."

His grumpy order has the wildest effect on me, flooding me with desire. I do as commanded, and drop my panties, too, feeling absolutely shameless. Angry sex with Liam is pretty damn appealing right now.

We're both starved for it, and since we recently had a little chat about my birth control pills, there's no need to slow down. I hear the sound of a zipper and then his mouth crashes down on mine again. I wrap my arms around his body just as I'm yanked into the air. My back hits the door as I wrap my legs around his waist.

But this isn't a movie so Liam struggles to line us up correctly. We're shaking and frantic. I lift myself up a little higher on his body and then finally—sweet relief as he fills me.

"Fuck...yes," he grunts between kisses. "Hold on. Bumpy ride head."

"Stop talking! Go!" I gasp.

Our teeth click together as he thrusts. If our relationship is really just sex, then we're doing pretty well right now. We're having angry, sweaty, crazy sex up against Liam's front door, and it is the best thing ever. Liam doesn't need to flatter me. I don't need him to tell me I'm still pretty, or that he likes my dress.

The truth is that you just can't fake this level of enthusiasm. Liam doesn't have to use words to tell me I'm sexy. I can hear it in each desperate sound he makes, and from the rough way he's taking me against the door.

"Oh, yeah. Oh fuck," he pants into my mouth. "Right now. Need you. Give it to me."

Need you. Those are the words that take me over the finish line. His voice is so raw, the words so bare that I lean my head against the door and shudder against him.

Liam makes a noise that's bone deep and desperate. Then all his muscles lock up as he gives one more hard thrust. That one might leave a little bruise, actually.

Totally worth it.

He lets out a moan that's so low and long that I wonder if the whole neighborhood heard it. Then his forehead goes *thunk* against the door and everything goes quiet, except for my raging, ragged heartbeat, which needs another minute to calm down.

We don't say a word for a little while, and Liam doesn't set me down. I use a limp hand to ruffle the slightly sweaty hairs at the back of his neck.

"Fuck," he whispers. "I'm sorry to be so…"

"Hot?" I finish.

With a weary groan, he gently sets me down onto the floor and disengages. "Unruly. That's what I was going to say. Or maybe *insane* would cover it," he mumbles.

"I don't know," I whisper. "I don't think I'd refer you to professional help just yet. Although another run-in with Decker could put anyone over the edge, I suppose."

"What did you see in him?" Liam asks. "Serious question."

I shake my head. "Nope. Not talking about him when I'm half naked in your entryway." I glance around. "Nice place you got here."

Liam cups my face in his hands. "Are you okay?"

"Absolutely. I'm more worried about you."

"It's nothing a seven mile run can't fix."

"That's your favorite stress relief."

He tucks a bit of hair behind my ear. "My second favorite. Right after trips to the hardware store."

"I don't know if we can keep this euphemism alive," I say. "It's a little dorky to always say we're running out to the *hard*ware store."

"Well the *hard*ware store is always open for you." He pulls me into a hug, and I lean against his chest and sigh.

His *hugs*, ladies. They're incredible. "Let's go back and talk my sister into taking that apartment."

19 EVERGREEN SPRINGS ETERNAL

Liam

DURING THE WEEKS THAT FOLLOW, I'm really restless. I don't know what my problem is. I've lost weight on account of all the running I've been doing. And Sadie and I have several additional frenzied fuckfests.

It feels like we're running out of time. Maybe because we are.

I've only got another couple of weeks at the daycare. They're interviewing candidates who might serve as my replacement. Nobody who's come in so far seems like a good fit, though. The hiring isn't up to me, but all three women who've applied for the job seem a little too flaky.

During nap time I sit quietly in the rocking chair and watch Amy's small back rise and fall as she sleeps. I mean—what if they hire someone who lets another child steal Piggypoo? Or what if they hire someone who won't keep track of Kate's helmet, or who doesn't notice when Blade is eating the playdough?

I feel anxious thinking about it. Time for another run after work.

Most nights—if I'm not with Sadie—I read research documents or study maps of Rome, trying to picture myself living there. I make note of the best cafes and the best gelato shops.

Somehow I don't think I can get excited about gelato if I'm eating it all alone.

Sadie only says enthusiastic things about my upcoming trip. "All those monuments," she says to me one night as we chat on the phone. "I need a picture of you at the Coloseum. I miss traveling."

I grit my teeth when she says things like that, because the subtext is that she's moved on to another stage in life, while I'm still a kid traipsing around Europe for fun.

Been there. Done that. Woke up on a park bench in Amsterdam with my wallet missing. My research trip is a little less frivolous, and only slightly less temporary.

"Traveling is fun," I admit. "But mostly I'll be at the lab, coding in the experiment results, so we can get a lot done in a short time."

"I know," she says gently. "Though I hope you will have fun."

There's a silence on the line then, because we always stop short of discussing next spring, when I'll move back home again.

Sadie treats our relationship like it has an immutable expiration date. She seems to like it that way. And I can't bring myself to ask why.

"There's a party for my dad," I say instead. "It's the night of his primary election. I've been meaning to ask if you'll come with me as my date."

"A family party?"

"Yeah." I sigh. "I can't promise excitement. Unless you're a huge fan of shrimp cocktails and geezer music. But I'm supposed to bring a date and there isn't anyone else I want to ask except you."

"I'll go. I'm happy to, so long as Decker can babysit. Tell me the date."

The knot in my chest dissipates because Sadie said yes to

family dysfunction and country club food. She said yes to standing at my side even though she knows my father is a dick. She didn't even have to think about it. It was almost a reflex.

She likes us! fourteen-year-old Liam squeaks. He always looks on the bright side.

"Mark your calendar for August twenty-first."

"I'll let Decker know right away," she says, and my heart grows another size larger. "What's the dress code?"

"Low cut and lots of skin."

"Liam!"

"Sorry," I snicker. But Sadie could go naked and she'd look perfect to me. "Sadly, the dress code is Country Club on a summer night. I'll be wearing a navy blazer with gold buttons and a boring tie that matches my brothers.'"

"That's very obedient of you."

"Isn't it?" I'll wear what the man wants to his stuffy party, but it's about the only thing I'll cave on. Not my job. Not my attitude. But he can have the tie to celebrate his primary victory. "Thanks for coming with me, hot stuff. It means a lot to me." She might as well know.

"It will be my pleasure," she says.

"I'll make sure of that afterwards," I promise, and she laughs although I'm dead serious.

––––––––

But when the day comes, I'm not ready. I mean—I'm physically ready, in my boring outfit and striped tie.

I'm excited as always to spend an evening in Sadie's company, but I'm worried that my dad will be an ass to us somehow. I don't mind having my own life choices questioned, but if he gives Sadie even a little grief I might lose my mind.

Driving over to her house, I try to focus on the good stuff. Decker is taking the girls for the whole weekend. I've rented a hotel suite in the VanHeimlich building downtown. We'll be on our own. No Meg—who's still living at Sadie's until her lease starts on September first. No parents. No exes.

Sadie doesn't know it yet, but she's getting another massage from Sven/Kevin tomorrow, and Sadie and I will spend the rest of the time having sex and eating room service.

Our summer together will go out with a bang. So to speak.

I've spent the day trying to decide which parts of her to worship first. The suite is on a high floor, so I'll undress her while the downtown skyline shimmers all around us.

Now *there's* a happy thought to get me through dinner.

I'm running about ten minutes late, which is unlike me. I've studied enough psychology to know that it's probably my subconscious's fault. I don't want to go to the dinner, so I got ready too slowly.

But that's okay. Our plans include a cushion—a window of time between when the guests will arrive and when Dad turns up to act surprised. I'll just swing by, grab Sadie, and zip over to Evergreen Springs.

The party planner said that nothing ever goes wrong at Evergreen Springs, and since she's worked there since the wooly mammoth walked the Earth, I figure she ought to know.

That's when I pull down Sadie's block and spot black smoke pouring out of her kitchen window.

My heart leaps into my throat, and I slam on the breaks so hard there's a screeching sound. I'm out of that car in a flash and running for the back door. "Sadie!" I shout, and my throat is tight with fear. Images flash through my mind, of Sadie trying to escape from a second floor window with one twin under each arm.

"It's okay," she says quickly from the vicinity of the back porch. I spot her as I round the corner. She's standing outside with the girls. "I burnt some grilled cheese on the stove. But the fire is out already. The range is a mess from the extinguisher, but that's the worst of it."

I can't even reply for a second because I feel suddenly shaky. The smoke is dissipating quickly, and I hear the hum of what must be a fan that she's got on in there to clear the air.

"Wiam!" Amy darts forward and grabs my leg. "Grilled cheese burned all up."

I reach down and pluck her off the porch to give her a squeeze. When I stick my nose in her silky hair, it's smoky. Like a burnt marshmallow. "Are you sure you're okay?" I croak.

"We're fine," Sadie says gently. "Except for the obvious—I can't go with you tonight."

"Wait, what?" Shock has made me completely forget that I was on my way to Dad's shindig. But now I take in a few more details. Sadie isn't wearing a dress, she's still in cutoff jeans and a little T-shirt. And—more crucially—her shitbag of an ex-husband isn't here to mind the kids. "Where's D—" I stop myself just before saying his name, so the girls don't hear the question.

That's when I notice her red eyes and the mascara that's run down onto her cheeks. She gives me a weird smile; she's trying to hold herself together. "He can't make it," she says with a singsong voice. "He and Honey are in Aruba."

"Aruba?" I ask. I'm really confused. It's Decker's weekend with the kids. Why the hell would he take off for Aruba?

Oh right, because he's a shitbag.

But Sadie is trying to tell me something. She makes a very sexual hand gesture. She's made a hole with the fingers of one hand, and she's jabbing the other one through it repeatedly.

This is a very awkward game of charades. Decker is fucking... Aruba? Fucking Honey in Aruba?

And then I understand. The finger gesture Sadie's making isn't sexual. She's trying to mimic putting a ring on a finger. Honey and Decker are in Aruba *getting married*. "Married?" I mouth.

Sadie nods.

"Eloped," she mouths back. "A few days ago. I just got the call a half hour ago, though." She makes a crabby face.

Well, shit. I look her over again. Those red eyes look sad. Maybe it's because her ex moved on so quickly, or maybe because he bailed on his daughters *again*.

"I'm really sorry about tonight," she says, and her eyes water again. "I was really looking forward to the whole weekend."

Oh. Maybe it's *me* she's sad about. It's not about her ex's marriage? I don't even think—I just step forward and hug Sadie. Amy is sort of pinned between us, but she doesn't mind.

"Me too," grunts Kate from the floor. So I reach down and let her scale me like a tree. The girls are attached like boa constrictors to my arms and we all hug Sadie together.

Sadie sniffs and hugs us back.

"It's okay," I whisper. The girls pat her back, too.

"I *wanted* to go. I have the perfect dress and everything. But I can't just leave the girls..."

"Meg?" I suggest hopefully.

"Oh! Meg got a job waitressing. And she has a shift tonight. At least she's moving out next weekend. And I can't ask Brynn and Tom to watch the girls because little Zachary is still so small...and Ash and Braht always have weekend plans..."

I'm not doing a lot of clear thinking tonight. I'm on some kind of emotional overload, possibly caused by grilled cheese smoke inhalation. For whatever reason, my mouth is not connected to my brain right now, so I blurt out, "We'll bring the girls with us!"

Sadie is silent for a second. "To your dad's black tie surprise party at Evergreen Springs? The adults-only party?" Her expression suggests that I've lost my mind.

And maybe I have because I say, "Sure, it's not a big deal."

"Party!" cries Kate.

"Piggypoo?" says Amy.

"Yes!" I agree, feeling both happy and reckless. There's no way I'm leaving Sadie and the girls sad and lonely in a smoky house with no dinner. "Sadie, you finish getting ready." She definitely needs to redo that mascara. "And I'll pack the girls a bag. Helmets. Stuffed animals. Bribery items."

Sadie smiles at me through her tears. "I'll find some size-two dresses. We can at least try to look the part." She runs off, through the smoky kitchen and upstairs.

This is going to be fine, I think. My dad will be too busy glad-handing to care that I've brought a plus three instead of a plus one.

We shall all eat steak and scalloped potatoes, congratulate the old man, and then come back here to clean up Sadie's stove.

Funny how that sounds like a lot more fun than it really should. It's not just Sadie that I've fallen for, but the whole family.

I shove that thought far, far away, and go in search of Kate's helmet and the diaper bag.

————

We're only a half hour late. Okay, forty-five minutes. I've missed the setup hour, but I'm sure the country club has got it handled. That's why we're paying them the big bucks.

The moment I cut the engine of Sadie's car, we hustle the girls out of their car seats and run awkwardly inside.

My siblings meet me at the entrance to the Double Bogey room with frantic "Where have you beens?" and "What took you so longs?"

But a quick glance around the crowded room reveals that my father isn't here yet. So I'm counting it as a win.

"Are you on fire?" my sister Cassidy asks when I lean in to kiss her cheek. "You smell crispy."

"Long story!" I say cheerfully.

"And, uh, who's baby is that?" Aiden asks.

"Not baby," Amy whispers around her pacifier.

"Kids, you remember Sadie Mathews, right? She cleaned up

your messes for an entire summer fifteen years ago. And this is Kate and Amy, who are big girls. Not babies."

My siblings blink at Sadie for a second.

"Oh, wow," Cassidy says eventually. "Hi! Liam had the *biggest* crush on you." Then she slaps a hand over her mouth. "Whoops."

"That's, uh, old news, Cass." Although my neck feels hot under my shirt collar, suddenly.

"Nice to see you again," Cassidy says, shaking Sadie's hand.

"When did you become so beautiful?" Sadie asks, making my sister smile. "I mean, you were cute at seven, but now you look like you belong on the cover of a magazine."

Cassidy blushes. "Can I hold your daughter?"

Sadie hesitates, because Kate is sometimes volatile, and I know she's hoping this evening will go smoothly.

"Hold this one," I say, passing her Amy. "Just don't lose the pig, or we will cut you." Then, to relieve Sadie's burden, I take Kate in my arms, allowing Sadie to greet my brothers.

"Aren't you adorable?" Cassidy coos as Amy rests her head on my sister's shoulder.

"So what did I miss?" I ask my brothers. "Is the old man on his way?" I scan the room again and notice that it's a good showing. There must be a hundred people here, to celebrate the primary election victory of a circuit court judge?

My dad has a seriously large ego.

"I got a text a minute ago," Aiden says. "Stand by for a call."

"A call?" I boost a squirmy Kate a little higher up on my hip.

"Yeah, he wants to..." Aiden is cut off by the squeal of his phone. The ringtone is "I Did It My Way," which means our dad is calling him. "Guys, step over here, okay? We can at least try to uphold the illusion that this is a surprise."

My brothers and I huddle against the wall and Aiden taps the phone to start a video call. "Boys!" my father bellows. "Are you wearing the ties? We're two minutes out."

"We're wearing them," Aiden sighs.

166

My dad squints at the screen from the leather seats in his chauffeur-driven car. "Fix your collar, Connor," he barks. "And Liam, put down that baby. Why is there a baby at my party?"

"NOT baby!" Kate yells at the screen, making my brothers bite their lips to avoid laughter.

"Put it down," Dad repeats. "A baby with a helmet? Is there something wrong with that kid? Liam always has to fuck something up."

"Bad words!" Kate squeals, and my brothers lose their fight against convulsive laughter.

But I don't see what's so funny. "Dad, you told me to bring a date," I say frostily. "We had a babysitting issue, so I brought three. When you get here you can tell Kate how pretty she looks in her dress." I'm not taking *any* shit from him tonight. He might as well know up front.

His eyes narrow. "We'll speak later. If you ruin this night for me, I will never forgive you."

It's a threat I've heard many times before. There's already about a million things he'll never forgive me for already. What's one more? "Dad," I say quietly. "If you're rude to my guests, I won't show up wearing the right tie and suit coat again. I won't show up at *all*."

My father's mouth forms a snarl. "That's some gratitude. You have sixty seconds until I walk into that room." He ends the call.

"Bad man," Kate mutters. She tugs on the strap of her helmet.

"He's just hungry," I lie. "If we all yell 'surprise' at the right time? There will be good things to eat."

"Yummies," Kate agrees.

"Yeah. Yummics."

I'm interrupted by Sandy the party planner. She's ringing a triangle. An actual triangle! Like she's calling the cows home to the barn. "Thirty seconds!" she yells. "Places everyone!"

The crowd hurries to reassemble itself. Men in suits and women in dresses that are fancy yet somehow impeccably dull all scramble to find a hiding place. This is not a young crowd. There's a banner that says, "Congratulations, Judge!" The tables are set, the band's in place, and the TV is on to announce the primary results.

Sadie and I set the girls down, because they're getting squirmy.

Sandy stops ringing the triangle and shouts at us "QUIET, EVERYONE! HUNKER DOWN!" I'm perplexed by the yelling. And there's nowhere to hunker down to, so everyone in the Double Bogey room just sort of squats.

The girls watch with wide eyes as all the other adults crouch down to hide. I wonder what they see, because to me they look like a bunch of old people trying to surf in dress clothes, with no boards or water.

I wave Sadie closer to me. "Don't worry about hiding," I counsel her. "Just stand here with me." I refuse to hide from someone who already knows I'm here. And this tie is choking me, so I reach up and loosen it a little.

Fuck it. If my father can't handle a loosened tie on his eldest son, then I really don't care.

All eyes are on the door. Amy is nervously sucking on her pacifier and hugging Piggypoo so hard I'm afraid she's going to pop off its head. Kate is standing between my feet, and she's actually revving in place. I reach down and clutch the bow on the back of Kate's dress, to steady her. This is a lot of stimulation for the girls. Probably too much.

It was selfish of me to bring them here. I just really wanted Sadie at my side. It's not the most relaxing moment to hang out with my family, but I wanted her near me. And Sadie's girls are part of Sadie's life, and I want them in my life too.

Permanently.

This is a lot of realizations all at once.

Then things start happening very fast.

There's a wheeze as the doors open on a blast of hot outside air, meeting the chill of the arctic indoors.

Everyone leaps forward, and their collective screams of "Surprise!" are deafening. The sound is so loud that Amy lets out a terrified wail. And then suddenly I'm holding only the bow of Kate's dress in my hand. Kate has launched herself forward. She's running toward my father.

I can only watch the rest of it as if in slow motion.

Dad is waving to the crowd like he's the president and not just the winner of a thinly contested local judicial primary. While Kate, head down, helmet in place, is charging like a bull, right for him.

"Oh no, she's...!"

Sadie doesn't even get to finish the sentence before it happens. Even over the din, I can hear the impact of Kate's helmet to my dad's crotch.

His "Oomph" is audible followed by a slow motion crumpling to his knees and then the fetal position.

I'm not sure what I'm supposed to do in that moment. They didn't teach this in the graduate program for child development. But I'm pretty sure my reaction isn't standard operating procedure, anyway. I don't run across the room and comfort my father, or grab Kate for a discussion of Meaningful Consequences.

I only lean over to Sadie and whisper with awe, "Kate is going to make a *terrific* linebacker."

20 THE PREPPY LOBSTER

Sadie

"UH-OH," Amy says in a singsong voice.

It's the understatement of the century. Liam's father is lying red-faced on the plaid carpeting, making bleating noises like an injured sheep. Wellwishers swarm, and someone grabs for Kate.

But my daughter darts past outstretched hands and comes flying back to me. I scoop her up off the floor and she buries her face in my shoulder. This actually hurts, because that helmet is quite hard.

Just ask soon-to-be Judge McAllister.

"Bad man," Kate says.

"That bad man is Liam's father," I whisper. "You're going to have to say you're sorry."

"No," Kate says.

Ah, well. She's two. What did I expect?

"Everything will be fine," Liam murmurs, but I'm not sure if he's trying to reassure himself or Kate. Or me. "He kind of had it coming."

Be that as it may, I don't think we'll be welcome here. "I'm going to put the kids in the car and go," I say, taking a sidestep toward the door. "I think it's for the best."

"Hungry!" Kate says, perking up. "Yummies. Now."

"I promised food," Liam says. "Look, the passed hors d'oeuvre have started." He gestures toward a young waiter carrying a tray of something around the room.

"Liam," I whisper. "This isn't the right place for us."

His kind blue eyes meet mine. "I know, Sadie. I made a major miscalculation. But that doesn't mean I'm going to put two hungry girls in their car seats and send them home to a blackened kitchen. Give me ten minutes to congratulate my father and we'll head straight for the nearest drive-through."

"Okay," I say softly. I'll do almost anything when he looks at me like that. Even drive-through.

The waiter approaches and Kate sticks one short arm out and nabs a crab cake off of it.

"Baby, I don't know if you like..."

Kate shoves it in her mouth and chews.

"Me too," Amy says, and the smiling young man leans forward so she can reach them.

"You'll need these, I think," he says, offering me napkins.

"Thank you."

Liam grabs two more crab cakes just before the guy leaves. Wordlessly, he offers these to my girls so they can each have another one. "There you go, ladies. Quite the sophisticated palate we're developing tonight."

He smiles at me, and my tummy tightens inside my dress. Liam is a real man. He's strong but kind. Smart but also sweet. He looks after my children and he looks after me, as often as I allow it.

I like him way too much.

"What do you say, girls?" I ask, my voice thick. Just because I'm having an emotional moment doesn't mean they can skip the thank-yous.

"Daddy?" Amy says.

Liam's eyes widen. Then he chuckles. "Well, that's very flattering, but..."

"Daddy!" Kate shrieks.

I feel a prickle of awareness at the back of my neck. Slowly, I turn my head. There's really no way that Decker's here. He's in Aruba, getting married!

But unless I've completely lost my marbles, that is Decker. And his new wife, Honey. Her massive diamond ring gleams beneath the fluorescent lights. It's practically sparking and spitting on her finger. *Mental note to revisit the child support Decker is paying.* If he can afford a ring like that, then he can afford to pay for the Tony Montessori preschool I'm eyeing for next year.

But why is Decker here? Did he even go to Aruba? And why is he stomping in our direction looking like an angry tiger? Seriously, his face is so red that I'm worried he might have a heart attack, fall down dead, and then be buried right outside by the water trap at hole 11.

As he gets closer, I realize he's sunburned. He's a tomato. That's going to hurt a lot in about twenty-four hours.

Serves him right.

"Uh-oh," say Amy and Liam simultaneously.

"Daddy grumpy," Kate warns just as he arrives in front of us. I notice that Liam has reached for my hand, and I close my fingers around his. I feel rooted. Like we're a team.

That's something else I'll have to revisit later, because Decker practically spits out his greeting. "What the hell was that?"

No hello. No, *gee, sorry I lied not two hours ago when I said I was still out of the country.* But then again, Decker never did learn to apologize.

I'm amazed that I was ever married to the preppy lobster in front of me. How did I let that happen? I don't have much time to contemplate it because Decker just keeps talking.

"This is an adults-only party. Kate *rammed* the judge! I've never been so embarrassed."

"Aspiring judge," Liam corrects under his breath.

"You're embarrassed, huh?" I ask. My voice gets high and crackly when I'm angry. And I'm angry. "You *should* be embarrassed about your poor record of showing up when you say you're going to, and generally giving a crap about the people who depend on you."

Behind him, Honey flinches. Then she looks down at the sparkling bauble on her finger and seems to tune me out.

"Ah," Decker says, waving a hand dismissively. "So I might've fudged a little on the details of when I was back in town. I just didn't want to complicate things and since I had plans, it seemed easier to let you keep the girls just a smidge longer."

"A smidge," I bark. "A smidge is fifteen minutes. Or maybe a couple of hours. But the last time you saw them was two weeks ago. You have two children. I am already over the fact that you broke your promises to me. But I won't let you do it to them."

Decker has the good sense to look briefly ashamed. Or maybe it was just a trick of the light, because a waiter leans into our unhappy little party and offers us champagne. Decker's face lights up immediately and he plucks one off the tray.

And what a dick. He takes a sip immediately, instead of getting a drink for his new wife.

"Aren't you going to offer some to your new wife?" I ask because I'm not in the mood to let things go. And Honey is still sort of hovering behind him looking nervous. God help me but I feel so sorry for this woman. She has to go home with Decker for the rest of her life, unless he trades her in for a new model.

"Uh, no," he says with a nervous chuckle.

"I can't have champagne," she says. "Because..." She slams her lips together.

"You've got to be kidding me," Liam says, plucking two glasses off the tray and handing one to me.

And then it sinks in what Honey means. "You're...p—" I catch myself just in time. I don't know if Kate and Amy know what pregnant means, but I do not want to explain their new sibling to them until I have ten seconds to get used to the idea.

But now their sudden wedding makes so much more sense.

"We'll talk about it later," Decker snaps. "In private. Not in front of your babysitter." Decker gives Liam the once-over.

"I have a name," Liam says. "Hold this, baby," he says to Amy, handing her his wine glass. "But no sips. That's a grown-up drink." Then, his hand free, he offers it to Decker. "I'm Liam. We meet again."

"Liam," Decker says with a sneer. "The manny. Or have you been promoted? Are you now the pool boy she's fucking?"

"I don't have a pool," I say. And then, because I can't stop myself, "But he is very talented in the bedroom. It's been very educational for me."

Decker's eyes bulge, and is it my imagination, or does Liam flex his pecs under that ridiculous suit?

My ex-husband's disapproval is thick. Kate, who has wiggled her way onto the floor, now latches onto his leg. "Stop," he hisses at her, clearly irritated. "This is neither the time nor the place. I'm here to make an *impression*."

"Oh, you are," Liam says with a snicker. "Kate, here." He downs his bubbly and then sets the empty glass on a ledge beside us. Then he squats down a few inches so my other daughter can climb up, too.

Decker is going to have three children. Three. And the only decent father within a five-foot radius is the hot guy with no kids of his own. The universe works in mysterious ways.

And something else Decker said nags at me. "You're here to make an impression?" I ask. "On who?"

Decker glances toward the judge, who has recovered from his crotch strike and is shaking hands with all of his well-wishers. And then I get it. I'm standing in a room full of the most successful lawyers in town. Decker is prospecting for new clients, and the Honorable McAllister has lots of rich friends. "Oh, wait." I say. "Are you here to meet Judge McAllister?"

"Not that it's any of your business, but yes, Sadie. I've been trying to connect with him. And Honey is a member of this club. It's just kismet, don't you think? So please keep the girls occupied, will you? I don't want them ruining this for me."

I am not a violent person, but I feel violent right now. Decker doesn't even care that his daughters are listening to every crass thing he says.

Not until I started spending time with Liam do I realize how bad he really is. How arrogant and ungrateful.

"So, you want to meet Mr. McAllister?" Liam says.

Decker looks at him like Liam is something he wiped from the bottom of his shoe. "What do you care, Pool Boy?"

Then I smile because I know what's coming. And it's beautiful and terrible all at once. I give Liam a slight nod. *Go on.* We're in this together.

"Hey, Dad!" Liam calls. "Someone wants to meet you!"

The look of sheer panic that Decker expresses erases all my violent tendencies. He's just slowly made the connection that the man he's insulted is the son of the man that he needs to impress.

It's a beautiful thing. I want to high-five Liam, but that would be too obvious. So maybe I'll just give him a blowjob later instead.

I need to stop thinking about Liam and his dick in my mouth, because his dad is walking (limping) over and I need to look like A Very Appropriate Girlfriend.

"Liam," Phil McAllister says in a gruff voice. "What is the meaning of this...chaos that nearly ruined my victory party?" He squints at his son, who's holding both the perpetrator and her twin sister in his hunky arms.

"Funny you should ask," Liam says calmly. "This man would like to apologize to you for that. Meet Decker Mathews. He'd like

175

to explain why his daughters are here tonight and not at home with him as he'd promised."

"Uh, um..." Decker sputters. "Well, mrgggt!"

I stare at Decker, wondering if he's actually choking on something. As much as I loathe him lately, I'd still give the father of my children the Hug of Life if necessary.

"See, it's...*urrgh*." Decker turns a darker shade of red, which is now approaching purple. But he isn't choking on food. Only on humility. "I needed...brrrrgh."

"He didn't want to miss your victory party," Honey says, leaping to her new husband's rescue.

"Do I know you?" Phil demands.

"Not yet, sir," Decker manages. "Nrrrgh. I mean, congratulations." He holds out his hand, which a confused Phil McAllister shakes.

"Thank you. And see that it doesn't happen again." He frowns deeply, then reaches out to adjust his son's tie. "Ah, there. That's perfect. And I see the buffet table is ready." He strides off.

"More yummies!" Kate yells.

"Food," Amy demands.

"We'll make a plate for each of you," Liam promises. He sets the girls down. "Get in line, okay? No pushing, no cutting." They sprint away.

Decker just stands there looking at the back of Phil McAllister's retreating form. He looks like he might cry.

"You're dismissed," I tell Decker, because he seems a little stuck.

His shoulders slump. "I've been trying to meet that man for years."

"He's not an easy one to spend time with," Liam says cheerily. "Ask me how I know. I'd try the golf course next if I were you. He also enjoys adults-only cruises."

"I love those!" Honey beams.

Liam just shakes his head.

"Should I, uh, take the girls home?" Decker asks quietly.

It takes a full beat to process the question, because it's so unlike him. "Right now?"

He nods.

"Well, do you have two car seats, diapers, and extra clothes?"

He shakes his head.

"How about next weekend instead?" Liam asks. "Because I just promised them food, and I always keep my promises. Actually, they're almost to the front of the line. Excuse me." Liam trots off to ward off disaster. I don't think he even realizes he still has a stuffed, pink pig under one arm.

I watch him go, feeling wistful. I love him so much. I really do. I'm already over our age difference. I'm over believing that I'm not young enough or thin enough or C-section-scar-free enough for him.

If only he were mine for keeps.

"Next weekend, then," Decker says with a sigh.

"If you blow off our girls, I will notify my lawyer," I say, turning my attention back to his sun-crisped face. "They were your kids first. I won't let you push them away."

"Right," Decker says, looking grumpy again. My threat won't sit well with him, but I need him to know I'm serious.

"We're buying a house," Honey says helpfully. "They'll have a room with bunk beds."

"No bunk beds until they're five," I snap. "Unless you want to spend a lot of time in the E.R. I mean, have you *met* Kate?"

"Twin beds, then."

I sigh and turn to Honey. "Congratulations," I say carefully. "I hope you're feeling all right." I'm not going to alienate this woman. She's in way over her head, but Kate and Amy and I don't need to make any enemies.

"Thank you. It was, um, unexpected." She gives me a nervous smile.

I try not to flinch. I don't know how this turns out for either of them. But it isn't my drama. "Still a blessing!" I say with forced cheer. "And you can learn more about toddlers next weekend when my girls show up to entertain you both."

"Looking forward to it," Honey says, sounding about fifty percent convincing. "Shall we go home, Decker?"

"Yeah," he says, looking tired. "I can shmooze another night. I'll be along in a second, okay?"

Honey takes the hint, bidding me good night and then walking away.

"That was, uh, nice of you," he says. "I mean, you were nice to Honey."

I was, wasn't I? "It's not her fault you're a shitty father. Do better, okay? I don't want to lawyer up, but I will if I have to."

Decker processes this for a second and he seems to accept it. "Got it," he says. "We'll, uhm, text about next weekend."

"Right. Later."

He walks away, and I head for the buffet line to dine with the three cutest people in the room.

21 SPARKLES EVERYWHERE

Liam

"'...AND then the sparkle princess asked her sparkle pony, 'What adventures shall we have today?' 'Sparkly ones!' replied the sparkle pony. 'Let's use the sparkle wand to scare up a spell!'"

It boggles my mind that someone actually wrote these words down on a page and called it literature. Maybe it's all just a sick joke to find out what parents will tolerate at bedtime.

Tonight that sucker is me. I'm in a rocking chair with two sleepy toddlers on my lap. This is my second pass through the book, and both Kate and Amy's eyelids are appropriately heavy. The sparkle princess uses her sparkle wand to save the kingdom, and the girls' eyelids droop even further.

It was a hell of an evening. After Kate's run-in with my father's balls, and after Sadie's run-in with Decker, and after I forced that fucker to apologize to my pompous father, we all ate our weight in steak and scalloped potatoes. Who knew that drama worked up such an appetite?

But as soon as everyone had eaten, I was ready to get the heck out of there. So I approached Sandy, the party coordinator, and asked if I could get two congratulatory mini cupcakes before they were officially served. "I know two little girls who need to go home to bed," I'd said, pulling the kid card.

"Why, absolutely!" she'd said. "We can't have them up past their bedtime, can we? Nothing ever goes wrong at Evergreen Springs."

I'm not sure my father's scrotum would agree. But he's the kind of man who always keeps up appearances. I'd spotted him holding court in front of the faux stone fireplace, pouring brandy from a snifter for his cronies.

Leaving Sadie at the table with the girls, I approached my father to say good night. "Well done, Dad," I said. "Congratulations."

"Thank you, son!" He beamed at me and then at his stuffy friends. "Liam, your date tonight is very attractive. But she looks a little familiar. Have I met her before?"

He'd floored me, because I couldn't believe he'd remember. "You hired Sadie to babysit us the summer I was fourteen."

"Oh," he'd said with a faraway look in his eye. "Indeed. I always thought that girl was a looker."

That gave me an honest-to-god shudder. "Hey now. If you perv on my girlfriend I won't invite you to our wedding."

My dad had laughed, as if I were making a joke.

I wasn't.

And it's funny to realize how easy it is to admit that I want to marry Sadie. There's something to think about later.

Now we're safely back at Sadie's house. When we'd pulled into her driveway, there wasn't any discussion about whether or not I could come in for the night. I didn't ask, and she didn't object when I pulled my overnight bag out of the trunk to carry it inside.

"You want bedtime duty or to clean up the smoky kitchen?" I'd asked her.

Sadie had only given me a grateful smile. "It's storybook time, now that you mention it. *The Sparkle Princess* is waiting upstairs."

I give her a meaningful look. It's half *I want to get you naked*, and half *you owe me for mentioning that evil book.*

"Wiam read it," Amy had demanded immediately.

And so here I am in the rocking chair, two sleepy girls in my lap. "And the sparkle pony lived happily ever after with the sparkle princess," I say, closing the book.

"More," Kate says, but then she yawns.

"That's all," I say lightly. "More tomorrow. And if you both go right to sleep, I'll make pancakes in the morning, I promise."

"Pancakes," Amy agrees.

"With faces," Kate adds on, always upping the ante.

"With faces, sure. But only if you're both super quiet now and go to sleep."

"Shh," Kate agrees.

I rock the chair one more time, just enjoying the stillness. Two small people are snuggling me. Who would give this up? That asshole Decker broke a family in two just so he could bang the nanny. And a year later he's married with another kid on the way.

For his own sake, I hope Decker learns what contentment looks like. Because it looks a hell of a lot like me right now.

"All right, ladies. Let's get in those beds." I set Kate down first, and she lies right down on her mattress, her diaper butt pointing at the ceiling.

Then I lay Amy on her mattress, tucking Piggypoo right beside her. The last thing I do before leaving the room is whisper "good night."

The house is so quiet when I leave them. I tiptoe downstairs, looking for Sadie. But the kitchen is clean, and she's nowhere to be found. So I walk back upstairs and peek into her bedroom.

And holy God. I am not prepared for the sight of Sadie lying naked on her back across the bed, one hand between her legs.

I'm hard before I can step into the room and lock the door behind me. "You started without me?" I ask, hurriedly unbuttoning my shirt and tossing it aside.

"Can't stop thinking about you," she whispers, and her bare breasts heave on a sigh.

"Is it because I made your ex look like a jackass?" My belt is next. I hurl it to the floor and unzip my trousers.

"That was fun," she admits. "But that's not even it. I love the way you just deal with whatever comes your way. You make the best of it and still have fun. Your attitude is even sexier than your pecs."

"You like my pecs?" That's what I got from that sentence. So I flex them for her. She licks her lips.

I'm so hard I can hardly get my underwear off. But somehow I manage. Then I'm naked and crawling on top of her. She starts to move her hand away, but I grab her wrist. "No, touch yourself. Nothing has ever made me so horny as seeing that. I love it when you're dirty, Sadie."

She moans as I go in for the kiss.

Then we're off to the races. Hot kisses and wandering hands. We roll around on her bed until we're both breathless and desperate for each other. I need her so badly. But somehow I find the willpower to pull back and stand up at the foot of the bed. "Roll over," I bark. "And move down here."

Sadie hurries to comply. And when I take her hips in both my hands, she moans. I nudge her knees apart with one of mine. "Wider," I demand, just because I can. This is the stuff of fantasies right here. In a month I might be sitting in the finest cafe in Rome, unable to notice the impressive scenery. Because I'll be deep inside my own head, remembering how soft she is in my grip, and how lovely she looks—her back rising and falling with each heated breath—as I bury myself sweetly inside her.

"Oh fuck, Liam, yes," she babbles at the quilt on her bed.

I take her in deep, measured strokes, trying to make it last.

Then I let go of her hips, dropping my chest to her silky back, my forearms caging her body. "You are so fucking beautiful," I whisper in her ear. "Don't ever forget that."

She gives a little sob of pleasure and I have to bite my lip to hold myself back. There's no condom between us these days. *This is everything*, a voice inside my head suggests. *It's too hot. Too perfect. We have to come now.*

Don't embarrass us, I want to reply. And then I realize—fourteen-year-old Liam isn't the voice I hear anymore. That kid has moved on. It's twenty-nine-year-old Liam who's so desperate he can't stand it. Desperate for release. And desperate to stay here as long as Sadie will have me.

We could make another baby right now, that voice suggests. *Or, you know, soon.*

I groan at the decadence of that idea. And now I'm losing this battle, so I slip a hand under Sadie's body and touch her.

"Yessss," she hisses. "Don't stop."

As if. Because I never want to stop.

———

We lay there in a happy heap on her bed afterward. I'm exhausted, but I can't stop kissing her on the neck. The jaw. The temple. "Sadie."

"Mmh?" she asks, stroking my chest.

"I gotta tell you something you don't want to hear."

Her gaze flutters up to mine. "What?"

She's sex-flushed and adorable. So I smile as I say it. "I love you. It's inconvenient but it's true."

"Liam," she breathes. "That wasn't supposed to happen."

"Oh, please. I never had a chance." I run a finger down her cute little nose. "I started falling before I got my driver's license. And spending two months in your company—and in your bed— didn't exactly scare me off."

Her eyes dart away from mine, and she clears her throat.

"You don't have to say it back," I whisper. I already know she isn't ready. But I've studied almost as much psychology as she has, and I also know she could love me, too. The way she smiles at me when I kiss her is a big clue. And then there's the wistful expression on her face when I'm holding her little girls.

"I don't deserve you," Sadie says softly.

"Sure you do. And I don't expect you to wait for me while I spend nine months in Italy. But you can bet I'm going to be desperate to check in on you the minute I'm back."

Sadie inhales deeply and then lets it out again. "I don't even know how to think about that. I don't even know what I'm making for dinner tomorrow, let alone in nine months."

"We're going out for dinner tomorrow, because I'm going to ask your sister to babysit. And I don't expect you to be thinking about me while I'm gone." I hope she will, but I won't burden her with my dreams.

"Liam," she whispers. "I love you, too."

"Wait, what?" I probably just hallucinated that.

She gives me a sad smile. "You're so amazing that you're probably too good to be true. But yeah—I'm a little bit in love with you. And I'm so grateful that we got to spend the summer together. You made me feel like me again."

My mind is pretty much blown. I never expected her to admit that our relationship is bigger than just sex and childcare. And I didn't blame her for protecting herself from feeling things for me.

I swear to God, I can't even speak right now. So I just kiss her instead.

22 LATE NIGHT HEARTACHE

Sadie

AT ONE IN the morning my eyes fly open. I lie there in the dark, trying to figure out what's wrong.

Oh. I'm alone in the bed. That's what's wrong.

I roll over, but the only sign of Liam is the way my sheets carry the scent of his skin.

Did he go home? I hadn't asked him to. I hope he didn't think I needed him to do that. We have so little time together, I wanted to make the most of it.

The pang I feel when I think about him leaving has me wide awake now. So I sit up and swing my legs over the side of the bed. My robe is on the chair, so I grab it and slip it on, and then tiptoe out of the open bedroom door and into the hallway.

All is quiet at the girls' door. So I continue to the top of the stairs, which is lit by the glow of a downstairs lamp.

I ease my way downstairs and into the living room, where I find Liam on the sofa, his adorable reading glasses perched on his phone as he taps on his iPad. "Everything okay?" I ask, causing him to startle.

"Jesus," he says, placing a hand on his heart. "I didn't hear you come downstairs."

"What are you doing? Can't sleep?" I move around behind him. His iPad has the email program open. He's writing a letter.

Dear Charles,

I too am an associate of the Child Study International program, headed to Rome next month. I noticed that you're slated for a research spot in Chicago, and I'm actually writing to ask if you'd have any interest in swapping places.

Liam catches me reading over his shoulder, and quickly lets the tablet fall face down on his chest. "Sadie, look..."

"Chicago?" I gasp. "Why would you do that? You're supposed to go to Rome."

He sighs. "I am going to Rome. Probably. But I was just reviewing my options."

"No," I correct him. "You were just making plans without telling me."

Liam cranes his neck to look at me. "Come here, would you? Sit down."

I bristle at the suggestion, which is ridiculous, because we clearly need to talk. But I'm experiencing rapid onset symptoms of fight or flight. And flight sounds really good right now.

"Please. Sit," he says again.

So I do the mature thing and march around the sofa to sit stiffly beside him. "You're supposed to go to Rome and learn Italian and ride a Vespa around the fountains." I try to say this firmly, but I might be a little on the emotionally wobbly side.

Liam actually laughs. "I've done that very thing, but it was in Prague. I love Europe, but I love you, too. So I was trying to figure out whether it's possible to stick around without blowing up my research fellowship."

Stick around. "Oh." I feel suddenly cold inside, so I pull my robe a little more tightly around my body.

Liam's face falls. "I see. You're looking forward to our expiration date, then?"

"No," I say quickly. "No, I'm not. But you can't just give up your trip like that. It wouldn't be right." I'm not looking to tie another man down before he's ready. Did that already. Have the T-shirt and the divorce papers to prove it.

"What if I *want* to stay, though?" Liam asks.

"No. You only *think* you do," I whisper. I've heard that before, too. "You're still in your twenties."

"Yeah, for about three weeks." He rolls his eyes. "I hate it when you say that. Like I couldn't possibly know what I want in life because I'm not as experienced as you are."

"Well, you're not." I have plenty of experience in these matters. All of it bad.

Liam puts the tablet on my coffee table and then props his forehead in his hands. "I don't know how to prove it to you, Sadie. I really don't. I want to be here with you and the girls."

I hear him say the words. And I hear in his voice that he means it.

But my stupid heart just can't believe it anymore. He'll feel trapped. He'll *resent* me. "I think you should go to Italy."

He lifts his head to stare at me. "Do you *want* me to go to Italy?"

No. Says my heart. "I think you should," says my fear.

For a moment we just stare each other down. This is like one of the horror movies I made him watch all those years ago. We already know there will be carnage, but we can't stop it from happening.

"Sadie," he whispers. "You know you're pushing me away."

I do know, but I can't help it. "Let's go to sleep," I beg. I didn't mean to have this conversation tonight. But the idea that Liam would change all his plans to be with little old me? It's bone chilling.

Because I know he won't be satisfied. I just *know* it. Decker wasn't satisfied and Decker's an ass. How could Liam, this beautiful, wonderful man, want to stick around? And for how long? A month? A year? It's not just me I'm fighting for here. It's not just my heart. I'm fighting for my girls too.

Liam pats the pillow on the end of the sofa. "I'm going to stay right here, I think."

"Why?" I blurt out.

He shrugs. "I can't just curl up in bed with you right now and pretend that everything is fine. But I promised to make pancakes in the morning. And I always keep my promises."

My heart gives a stab of pain. "Good night, Liam."

"Good night, love," he says.

My heart breaks right in two.

23 THE PURPOSE OF BRUNCH ISN'T THE BACON. IT'S THE EPIPHANIES.

Sadie

LIAM KEEPS HIS PROMISE. With the girls, he's terrific. He makes them each a gigantic pancake and let's them decorate the pancakes with fruit smiles, blackberry noses, and whipped cream hair. He is tender, and present, and involved.

You can't tell that anything is wrong, but it is. We're fighting. That silent awful fighting. He wants to stay and I want him to stay, but I'm forcing him to go. And I don't know why.

I do the only thing I can think of. I text my best friends. **Any chance you can meet me for emergency brunch in an hour?**

It only takes a moment before my phone glows with their response. **Yes.** and **Hell Yes.**

Once the pancake plates are rinsed and stacked in the dish washer, Liam grabs his bag, gives the girls hugs, and then turns to me. The way he's looking at me, I just...can't.

There's such disappointment in his eyes. I'm sure they're a reflection of my own.

He takes my hands in his, almost as if he's going to make a vow, and I get really nervous. "Sadie, I need you to really think about this. Not with your brain or your 'I should's' or anything, but think about it with your heart. I'm not your boy toy. I'm a man who loves you and your girls. We can make this work. I promise you."

Then he pulls me in for a kiss. It's deep and real and it's like he's speaking to me without saying a word.

I watch him pull out of the driveway and then realize that he made me a promise.

And Liam always keeps his promises.

I can't help the little smile that happens. It just does.

———

An hour later, my girls are at the trampoline park with Aunt Meg, and I'm with Ash and Brynn and baby Zach. Last time we were here together at Marie Catrib's, I was nursing both Kate and Amy, at the same time. This time, It's Brynn with the full boobs and a hungry baby. There's a little ache in me, missing that sort of closeness with the girls.

"Your nipples are humongous. They just pop right out." Ash is mesmerized. "I thought you said you had inverted nipples, though."

"I thought so too. Turns out sometimes you can make them pop back out. It just takes a long time hooked up to this vacuum-type machine."

"You call Zachary a vacuum-type machine? You need a better nickname." Ash takes a sip of her espresso.

Brynn and I share a knowing glance. We're both members of the breast pump club. We both know the secret handshake—it feels a lot like having your nipples twisted off. If Ash doesn't get the reference, neither one of us is going to clue her in and freak her out.

I've ordered tea and I'm letting it steep. Sort of the way I've been steeping myself. I'm only half-listening to Brynn and Ash talk about the mystery of inverted nipples. Even as I push my plate away, a feeling rises up inside my chest.

It's panic.

"I've fallen in love with Liam!" I blurt. "Not little love. Big love. Big, deep love. And he needs to go to Italy, but he wants to stay here with me, but if he stays and gives up his dreams, he's going to grow tired of me and the girls, and it will be Decker all over again, but worse, because I only loved the *idea* of Decker, but I love all of Liam. All of him."

Little Zach chooses that moment to let out an enormous burp. There's a pause and then the three of us start laughing, because burps are funny even when your future is uncertain.

"There was a lot packed into that statement," Brynn offers.

"Yep," I say. "I've been thinking about it a lot."

"Sooooo...let me get this straight. He loves you and he loves the girls and he wants to ditch Italy and stay here so...he can build a life with you?" Ash asks.

"Yes!" I cry.

"What a dickhead," Ash says. "I mean how *dare* that douchenozzle recognize how awesome you are and love you for who you are!"

"And don't forget the twins," Brynn says. "He's such a prick for loving them too."

"I know," Ash agrees. "Next time I see him I'm gonna grab him by the balls and give a twist. A little razzle dazzle of the old wrist, and those balls will spin right off."

"Serves him right for loving our friend."

I shake my head. I can't help smiling a little. When they put it that way, it does sound like I'm being ridiculous. I'm complaining because Liam loves me and he wants to commit to me and...what exactly is my problem? Why can't I jump in with both feet and no parachute? Why can't I let him love me?

Oh right, because that never ends well.

Brynn is squinting at me. "Here," she says. "Hold this."

"Oh, no!" I say. "No you don't!" But it's too late. Zach is already in my arms. He's been fed and burped and he's all soft and warm and sleepy. His little starfish hands are pulled up under his little chubby chin and...for a split second I see my own baby, a baby that looks a lot like Liam. And I can almost hear my girls playing with a dog in the backyard. Liam comes inside from lighting the grill. He smells smoky and I can feel his warmth before he even touches me. He moves around behind me, shifting my hair away from my neck, kissing the skin there and...

"You little shit!" I whisper to Brynn. "You did this on purpose!" I try to hand Zach back, but she won't take him.

"I just wanted you to think it through," she says. "To imagine a future with Liam."

"You never handed me a baby to see if I loved Braht," Ash says.

"Well, yeah. You hate babies. You don't want children. Also, I didn't have one handy. But I knew you loved Braht. If I wanted to prove it, I'd have put a stock portfolio in your hands with Braht's and your names on it."

Ash shivers with a frisson of sexual energy. "Oooh," she says.

"So...what do I do about this?" I ask, still confused. "I just let him, what, move in? Love me, love my girls. We get married. Get a dog. Have a baby together?"

Ash and Brynn look at each other. "Yeah," they say.

"But what does he get out of the deal? He'd have to give up his fellowship to Italy. Why would he do that? Why?" I keep asking because I really want to know.

Ash looks at me and says in her no-shit tone of voice, "What does he get out of the deal, Sadie? Seriously? Don't you know? He gets *you*."

I shiver again. "But Decker..."

Both my friends sigh. "Honey," Brynn says. "Decker wasn't the right man for you."

"I thought he was," I argue.

"Are you *sure?*" Ash probes. "Did you look deep into his weasel eyes and see a part of yourself reflected back at you?"

Decker's eyes aren't really weasel-like. But I let that slide. I close my eyes and think of Decker. I see a man who wants to rub elbows with lawyers at a golf club. I see the Decker who left me. I don't see the one I fell in love with.

Or do I?

It's been a long time since I gave any thought to why I fell for Decker. We'd been married for five years when he left me. But we'd been together for ten. I met him in my twenties, when I'd been a dorky psychology grad student. I was holed up in the library all the time, feeling like a nerd and a loser.

Decker was already graduating from law school, with several job offers. He was a preppy career man. I was drawn to his ambition and his confidence. Not to his shiny watch or his golf addiction. Those I overlooked. Because...

Wait. Why the hell did I overlook it?

"Goddammit." My eyes fly open. "I was drawn to Decker because I didn't think someone like him would ever find me attractive."

Ash smiles calmly. "And why was that a turn-on?"

"Because..." It's hard to admit this. "I felt like a boring nerd with vampire skin. And he was out in the world already making things happen. That seemed sexy. At the time."

"Hmm," Brynn says, and a little smile teases the corners of her mouth. "And now?"

"And now I realize that was shortsighted." And *stupid*. "Oh my God. I liked that he was shallow. I was sick of the emo boys who wrote me depressing poetry and talked about Freud all the time. Decker was a breath of fresh air."

"There's air between his ears, too," Ash mutters.

"Listen." I hand the baby back to Brynn, and this time she accepts him. "I gotta go." I pull out some cash and throw it down on the table.

"But we didn't do any of the real bonding activities yet," Ash complains. "Sit down. We have a whole plan for getting you drunk later and giving each other facials. I already bought the avocados."

"You two have fun! Love you both!" I grab my bag and then have Epiphany #3. I toss my car keys to Ash. "Can you drop my car off at my house? I have to run somewhere."

"Run?" Brynn asks. "You?"

I nod. I'm going to run, because I've just had an epiphany. And an epiphany like this one calls for an epic run, or at least a two-block fast-walk, straight to the man of my dreams.

24 WHEN YOU WANT SOMETHING, GO GET IT

Liam

I'M STANDING in my front yard staring at my house. I like this house. But I think it's time to sell. After all, I'll be away for months and months.

And after Rome, maybe I won't come back. Who needs this town? My father is going to be a judge. A little distance from that, and from him, might do me some good. My sister is going to live in the U.K. I should follow her lead. Stay in Italy after my research is done. There's just not much here for me anymore.

The house itself doesn't really feel like home. Maybe someone else can buy it and fill it with a wife and kids. "You deserve that," I say to my house.

"Come again?" says a breathless voice.

I turn around faster than the last living girl in the final act of a horror movie. And there is Sadie, standing on the walkway, looking sheepish. She's also looking a little sweaty and breathless. Her hair is mussed. Her skin glowy. It's a good look for her. "Hi," I say stupidly. I left her house only two hours ago, certain that we were finished.

And yet here she is.

"Hi," she echoes. Then she holds up a finger. "Just a second. I ran here, and...I don't. Do. That." I wait for her to catch her breath. She's got something to say to me and clearly it's important, or she wouldn't have run. Then she says, "It was my own damn fault."

"What?" I just blink at her. She's wearing cutoff jeans and a tank top, which is basically the first outfit I ever saw her wear. There's nothing fancy about it, but I swear she's more beautiful than any woman who ever graced the cover of a magazine.

"My marriage was a disaster," she says slowly. "But that's my own fault. I just realized that today."

"Wait, what?" I argue. "He cheated."

"He did," she agrees. "But do you remember my theory about plot twists and *Psycho?*"

This conversation is giving me whiplash. "Of course I do. I remember everything you ever said to me."

Sadie looks up at the sky for a moment and sighs. "I'm such an idiot. I really am."

"Tell me the thing about *Psycho*," I prod.

"Right," she says, beaming. "A plot twist isn't just about surprising the viewer. It's about the viewer surprising *himself.* At first you're half rooting for poor Norman Bates. He's trying not to be arrested for something his mother did. But then when you figure it out, it's shocking because..."

"You're rooting for the wrong character," I finish. I thought Sadie was a genius when she first shared this with me.

I still do.

"I was rooting for the wrong character," she says. "Decker was shallow. I knew that going in. You asked me what I saw in him, and I didn't answer you."

"Well..." I'm struggling to keep up with this conversation. "We were having sex. It wasn't good timing."

She grins. "The thing is, I have never found the right moment to think about this. Until today. But now I see it. I stuck with Decker because I wanted someone with expensive taste to like me."

"Why?" That doesn't sound like Sadie.

"Bad judgment," she admits. "Insecurity. Boredom. Take your pick. And it was fun for a while, so I didn't realize how badly things could go." She walks toward me. "They went pretty badly."

"Yeah. I get that." I stand perfectly still in the grass, wondering if Sadie is here to break up with me for good, or whether I have any hope that we'll come out of this together.

If I were a begging man, I would start begging right now.

"I chose badly the first time," Sadie says. "But I won't get it wrong again."

"That sounds like a plan," I say slowly. "You take your time figuring it out." I want to reach for her. I want to hold her for as long as she'll let me. But I won't pressure her. I tried that already and it didn't work. She's got to come to me on her own.

Sadie shakes her head. "I don't need any more time. I think I started falling for you the second you kissed me after our walk to the park. The girls were passed out in the stroller, and the sun was shining. And..." She swallows hard. "You're amazing, Liam McAllister. I love you and I'm sorry I've been such a head case."

She walks right up to me and leans her forehead against my shoulder. And then I just go for it—I cup her head in my hand and hold her against me. "I love you, too. Since I was fourteen. I know you think I'm going to stop, but my record so far is pretty good—fifteen years. You and me, we're going to be a forever thing. I promise."

"I believe you," she says. "But it's okay if you go to Rome first. And it's okay if you go to Chicago instead. You make your plans. I won't freak out."

"Not even just a little?" I stroke her hair. She feels so good against me.

"I'll try," she says. "And if I start to freak out you can just kiss me until I remember why we're making all these plans. Shouldn't take much. One kiss or two." She lifts her chin and smiles at me.

"Let's practice now," I say.

And then we do.

25 EIGHT MONTHS LATER

Sadie

I STRETCH OUT IN BED, the soft sheets woven around my naked body. There's a faint little knock on the bedroom door.

Okay, it isn't that faint. "LIAM!" Kate yells. "Get up now!" There's a knock again, only I'm pretty sure she's doing it with her helmet. She doesn't need that thing anymore, but now she wears it just for fun.

Ah well.

There's a chuckle from beside me in the bed. I reach over and run a hand across his abs. Sometimes I dream about these abs. And now they're here beside me.

Life is so very good.

"I'll get up," I tell him. "You sleep."

"Nope!" he says, sitting up. "I've been awake for an hour now. I'm jet-lagged. So I've basically been watching you sleep."

"That's creepy," I say with a yawn. "Or, at the very least, a waste of private time together."

He slides out of bed with a chuckle. "Don't you worry. I'll get you alone later. Besides, do you really think Kate is going to let me sleep in?"

"I guess not." If I got up instead, the girls would just stand outside the bedroom door and play loudly until their favorite person got up. They've missed him so much, too.

"Sleep in if you want," he says, pulling a pair of briefs over his attractive backside. "I'll keep the coffee hot."

"It won't be as good as an espresso in Rome," I warn.

He turns around and gives me a smile. "Maybe not. But the company is better." Then he takes three long strides toward the bedroom door and opens it up with a whoop. "Lordy! Who is this tall girl? And what have you done with Kate?"

I hear the kind of shriek that comes from being picked up and tipped upside down.

A few minutes later they've all gone downstairs without me. I can hear my girls chattering at Liam like a couple of magpies. Sleeping in won't happen for me, either. Not when all my people are downstairs.

I linger, though, lying perfectly still, listening to all their voices in the kitchen. It's funny to me how natural it is to have Liam here. And that this is now his home.

That part hasn't really sunk in yet, even though I spent the last few days rearranging the guest room to become his office. And I moved my closet around to make room for his things.

Last night I stayed up late waiting for his taxi to pull up in front of the house. The girls and I couldn't meet him at the airport, because his connection from Philadelphia was delayed.

I practically leapt up off the sofa when I saw headlights on the street. We survived nine months apart. Apart*ish*. There was a month at Christmas, a family trip to Euro Disney, and two separate little jaunts of my own to visit him in Rome.

It turns out that Liam and I are really good at keeping a long-distance relationship alive. Not having him here was hard, but it forced us to make time to just talk on the phone, and to work on deepening our relationship. We did this most weekdays at four. That's ten p.m. in Rome. I'd call him from my office, where there were no distractions. We talked about life, psychology, child development, Rome, and the girls.

Swear to God, Liam was more of a partner from 4600 miles away than Decker ever was.

I should really get up. But it's so comfortable here, thinking happy thoughts about my man...

My eyes pop open an hour later. Whoops. I guess I dozed off again. I've been really tired this week. My body feels like lead. It must be from all the reorganizing I've done.

I sit up and swing my feet off the side of the bed. My stomach gives a little lurch for no good reason. That's unexpected. Especially because there are good smells coming from downstairs now. I smell bacon and something sweet.

Pancakes? No. It's a cakey smell.

Mmm, cake. Liam is obviously getting a jump start on our party plans. We invited over our crew to have a laid back *Welcome Home, Liam!* barbecue. I already shopped for burgers and sausages, and Brynn is bringing side dishes, while Ash is tasked with bringing paper plates, booze, and bags of chips.

And Liam wanted to handle dessert. Which I'm smelling now. And the cake smells great.

Amazing, even.

I want it so bad, I'm actually drooling a little.

The only time I've ever craved cake is...

Uh-oh.

My heart rate accelerates. No. It can't be. But...it *could* be.

My face heats a little bit as I remember my trip to visit Liam last month in Italy while the girls were with their dad. It was pasta, pesto, and plenty of sex. Italy was a dream. And we didn't use protection, because I accidentally left my pills at home.

It seemed really romantic at the time.

Suddenly I am up, out of bed, pulling on underwear and yoga

pants and a sport tank. I've got to make a really quick errand to the pharmacy.

———

Liam

"Are you exhausted?" my brother Aiden asks me a few hours later.

I turn and give him a smile. "Why would you ask?" So far today I've baked a cake, mowed the lawn, and moved a bunch of furniture into the backyard. Also, I currently have Amy on my back while I'm hanging up Sadie's flower baskets on the front porch. But this party was my idea, so I knew what I was in for.

"Dunno," my brother says with a shrug. "Moving cross-country while jet-lagged and throwing a party."

"Eh. I'll sleep when I'm dead."

"Hopefully that won't be soon," my brother says, taking a swig of the beer I gave him. "Glad to be back?"

"You have no idea." My glance does a sweep of the yard, looking for Sadie. I'm hungry for another look, but she's in the kitchen setting up.

"This is the real deal, right?" my brother says, smirking at me. "Are you two going to get m—"

"Hush," I say, cutting off the question. There's a small person with big ears on my back. "If that's in the cards, I'd really rather discuss it with her, first."

I hope it's in the cards. But I push that thought aside for now.

"Are we having cake soon?" Amy asks from over my shoulder.

"Not before lunch," I say automatically.

My brother smirks. "Someone sounds like a parent already."

"How would you know?" I counter. Our actual parents never fed us lunch.

"Touché. Is there anything I can do to help?"

"Sure is." I reach behind my body and snag Amy. "Hold this. I need a quick shower before the others arrive."

Aiden looks taken aback as I place a preschooler into his arms.

"Tea party!" she says. "Come see my dollies' table?"

"Uh, sure."

I sprint for the stairs. The rest of our guests will start arriving at any minute.

"Liam!" Sadie says when I enter the bedroom. I'm already whipping off my sweaty T-shirt and aiming it at the hamper. "Oh, my. Carry on."

My gaze finds her in the walk-in closet as I unbutton my shorts. She's wearing a sleeveless dress, and her wavy hair is still damp from the shower.

Hey, little lady, my inner horny man says. *We could have a quickie right now and nobody would know.*

"Hey, little lady," I say, because apparently I have no self-control. Sadie and I had a lot of amazing conversations while I was overseas, but right around the moment the taxi pulled up to her house last night, my libido woke up and shook itself off like a hungry dog.

Her mouth opens and then closes again as I stalk toward her. "Hey, there's something I need to tell..."

She doesn't get the rest of the sentence out, because I've pinned her to the closet door with a kiss so hot that we might need the fire extinguisher. I'd like to keep going but there's the sound of a doorbell, and knocking, and then I just hear the door downstairs open.

"We brought booze!" I hear.

"Ash and Braht," Sadie says.

"Quit making out, you two!" Ash calls up the stairs. "I have some big news!" And just like that, Sadie has slipped out of my arms and away.

How did Ash know? Oh, right—Sadie told me all about Ash

and Braht and shenanigans in a pantry. So maybe she's just tuned into that sort of thing.

I take a deep breath and take a running leap for the shower.

———

It's chaos for the next few hours. Just after I make it downstairs, Brynn and Tom and chubby little Zach arrive. There are hugs and hellos, and the twins sweep in and grab Zach to "babysit." I'm pretty sure Kate means she's going to literally sit on him, but Amy and Piggypoo would never allow that, I'm sure.

Then there's a flurry of "Connor meet Brynn and Tom" or "Meg meet Cassidy" as my other siblings arrive and are introduced to Sadie's friends.

Cassidy and Meg seem to hit it off and immediately begin mixing cocktails while carrying on a steady stream of chatter over...I don't know what. I hear something from my sister about nudity and France and some guy named Jacque. I walk away from the two of them because a big brother just doesn't want to know.

Sadie is across the yard chatting with her friend Ash. I give her a longing glance, and I swear she gives me one right back. I want to whisk Sadie away—to the pantry, if necessary—and remind her how much I've missed her.

Score! my inner horny man cheers.

I give Sadie another meaningful look, and she smiles and starts to make her way over to me. Finally. But then Ash and Braht walk between us, deep in conversation and heading for the driveway. And when they're finally out of the way, I see my parents pop out onto the deck.

"My parents? Really?"

Sadie gives me a shrug. We'd talked about this before, the importance of second, and even second-hundred chances. But dealing with the 'rents while jet-lagged is a bridge too far.

Not like I have a choice. My dad approaches first, giving me an awkward one-armed man-hug. Now *that's* unexpected. The man doesn't do affection. I wonder if maybe Sadie is right—that my dad might want to mend things with me?

He's changed a bit over the last year. Softened up maybe. After he won his primary, it shocked him to lose the general election. And the loss seems to have a humbling effect on him.

Or maybe it was Kate's tackle to his nuts. One or the other.

"Nice house, dear," my mother says. "Sandie has nice taste."

"*Sadie*," I correct with a sigh. Two-hundred and one chances?

Then the door opens again and Ash leans out and hollers: "Our big news is ready to meet the public! Braht's brother Bramly just drove him over. Look who woke up from his wittle nap!"

Braht holds open the screen door and says, "Tada! We're puppy parents!"

"What are *puppy parents*?" my mother sniffs, and she and I might be on the same wavelength for the first time since...well, ever.

Ash and Braht descend the deck like royalty. And they're carrying more gear than most parents do when they drop their beloved baby off for daycare the first time. Braht is cradling an enormous dog bed, a designer bag stuffed with toys, a dozen bones—apparently the dog is teething—and a huge stuffed sloth. I have no idea what that last thing is for.

I squint at the two of them, wondering where the puppy is. Suddenly a big hairy monster charges, bolting right between Braht's legs. But this is not a puppy. It's a *beast*. It's a St. Bernard? It's moving so fast I can hardly clock his black, brown, and white fur. And there's a happily expending line of drool hanging from its furry jaw.

"Pony!" Kate chirps.

There is a collective gasp, and everyone leans back as the St. Bernard cases the yard, loping around, taking everyone in. I can almost see his doggy synapses firing as he zeroes in on my dad.

All I have time to think is: *not again*.

The puppy—the *beast*—charges right for him. But this time the family jewels are spared, since the dog leaps up on his long hind legs to slather my dad's face and neck with hot, goopy dog kisses.

It's quite disgusting, and I brace myself for violence.

But a miracle happens instead. My dad? He *laughs*. It's a weird, rusty sound, because the man never laughs. But I swear it's happening. And my mother even makes an awkward smirk. An attempt at a smile.

"Oh dear!" Ash says. "Sebastian, grab the monogrammed towel. We're prepared for this." A moment later he shoves a towel in my father's face, while Ash corrals the dog.

"Oh, babykins!" he says. "You're so cute when you get all kissy!"

"Sweet baby Jesus," Brynn says, patting the sleeping baby in her arms. "They have owned that dog for a day and a half and they've already lost IQ points."

"They have them to spare," Sadie says. Her arm slips around me and she snuggles in close. She drops her voice even further, leaning in to whisper in my ear. "We need to talk."

Yeah, we do. "You're not going to tell me we're getting a puppy, right?" I joke. And then I laugh.

But Sadie pales. "Not a puppy, exactly."

Well that's odd. Maybe she got a cat? I've never had a cat. ("Too much hair," my mother always said. "It's tacky.")

"Liam! The grill is hot!" my brother calls from the patio. "I need those burgers like yesterday!"

It's always something. "Coming!" I call over my shoulder. "Sorry, babe. Just need a minute. Then we'll catch up." I dash off to get the meat.

———

Sadie

The grilling takes forever, and I'm churning inside. Liam might freak out when I tell him my news.

Then I'll freak out, too.

You don't welcome home a man like this. *Hi, baby. Great to see you settling in. Eight months from now we'll have three kids under the age of four. So party while you still can.*

Not that Liam isn't culpable. He knew this could happen. But that didn't stop him in Rome. We got *so* carried away. It was glorious. But now I'm panicked. I know for sure that Liam wants another child. He said so several times.

But now he's getting one for Christmas this year.

Also, I'll probably have to have another c-section. Which means a new scar. On my naked body.

The only silver lining is that Kate and Amy will be *thrilled*. They are big fans of Decker and Honey's new bundle of joy, and they've been asking me to pop out another one.

"I can't do that, sweetheart," I'd said the first time Kate asked.

She'd given me an adorable little frown. "Course you can. Grow it in your belly."

Who knew my three-year-old would be ahead of the curve on this one? Not me. And it's not a comforting thought.

My sister is playing with my girls right now. She looks a little tipsy. Liam is turning burgers on the grill and laughing with his brother. Maybe I can steal him away for a second?

I feel like barfing, and not from morning sickness. It's nerves.

"Baby, would you get the condiments and the buns?" he asks as I approach.

"Buns," I echo. *Bun in the oven*, my subconscious taunts. "Coming up," I say with a sigh. "Faster than you think."

"Awesome," he says.

We'll just see if he's still saying that when I drop my bomb.

———

I don't get Liam alone for another three hours. It's not easy to get the guest of honor away from all his admiring fans. Eventually things start to cool off—the grill, the temperature, the party in general—I waggle my brows at Liam. I'm trying to say, "Come over here, big fella. I've got something to tell you."

He responds with a brow waggle of his own, then turns around and disappears.

Where did he go?

He's not on the deck with his relaxed and drunk parents. Not with Meg and Cassidy swinging in a giant hammock. Not with my besties and their men in the living room, where the twins are admiring baby Zachary as he sleeps in his bouncy chair.

Where is he?

I'm starting to panic a little when I reach the hallway and there's a tug on my arm. "Quick!" Liam says. "In here!" He pulls me into the bathroom and locks the door. It makes sense. It really is the only room in the house where you can get some alone time.

"I miss you," I say, because I do. It's not past tense: I *missed* you. No. It's present tense. I miss him being near me. I miss his hands on me. I miss his proximity and his presence.

"I'm here," he says. "I'm not going anywhere. In fact..." he says, just as I say, "I have something to talk to you about."

"You do?" *Crumbs.* "Maybe you better hear my thing first."

He opens his mouth to argue when someone twists the handle on the bathroom door. "Mama! I want another cookie!"

Before I can answer, Liam reaches up and puts a finger across his lips. His eyes are smiling at me.

I don't say a word.

"Mama?" Kate's voice demands. "Liam?"

Let's face it—I was going to say no to the cookie anyway. She's really not missing a thing right now if I stay hidden.

But there's no way to know if she's still out there, or if she's already given up.

Liam lifts his hands, silently asking me to tell him whatever I wanted to say.

I look up into his handsome face and smile. And he smiles back at me, warm and happy. We're hiding in a bathroom and our families are tipsy and there's a St. Bernard probably eating the living room furniture. But there's nowhere else I'd rather be right now.

Also, that look in his eye doesn't care about my c-section scar. I take a deep breath and relax. It's different with him. It just is.

I reach for Liam's hand, and lift my top a couple of inches. Then I place his palm on my belly. His eyes widen. He lifts his startled gaze to mine, and I nod.

Liam inhales sharply and then, as I watch, his eyes fill. But it's not sadness. It's the kind of happiness that can't be contained. It has to be released.

And still, no words are necessary as he presses his lips to my forehead and inhales deeply. His thumb strokes slowly across my belly, and I don't think it's possible to be any happier than I am right this second.

Then Liam wipes his eyes with the back of his hand and smiles. He holds up one finger in the universal sign for "shh." Then he takes *my* hand. He places it on his shorts. The man is hard. *Really* hard. And I tremble a little. I thought with the jet lag and all the ruckus, he wouldn't reach this level of readiness until at least a few extra hours of solid sleep. But as I flatten my palm over him I notice...that hardness...it has corners. It's a *box*.

A little square box.

Oh.

Oh my.

Now I'm tearing up. I know what he's going to ask, and he knows what I'm going to say, and we still don't need words. Words are all we had during our separation.

Now we just need action.

We kiss. Slow, and firm, and with promise. I don't know how

long we kiss. Long enough for Kate or Amy, or probably both of them, to pad away calling to Aunt Meg for a cookie. Finally, we part and Liam is smiling, and he's shaking a little when he reaches into his pocket, grabs the box, and opens it.

The ring. Oh! The ring is so beautiful I can't even believe it. It's platinum, with a cushion cut diamond. And it's *familiar*. The first time I went to Rome, we spent one magical night walking around and window-shopping. I'd stopped to admire the original handcrafted jewelry in one window. And I swear this ring was there.

But that was months ago! When I can finally speak I say, "Liam, have you been carrying this around with you for months?"

He brushes the hair from my face and looks at me. "I was just waiting for the perfect time."

Standing in our bathroom, huddled together secretly, while all of our loved ones are outside the door laughing or sleeping or chatting, and the girls ready to be tucked in, and our baby growing inside of me—this was what we've both been waiting for.

It isn't perfect at all. It's messy and chaotic, this love we have, the life we'll share. But it's ours.

THE
END

THANK YOU!

Sarina and Tanya appreciate your love and support! Visit us at
sarinabowen.com and tanyaeby.com.

7471

Made in the USA
San Bernardino, CA
11 September 2018